"Are you nervous?"

"No," she replied very quickly, in what  ded like a strangled v

She *was* nervous. just a guitar lesso

She nodded. "I kr

"So just relax and let me do the teaching." He settled his arm around her slender shoulders, and the scent of her fresh-smelling shampoo wafted his way, filling his senses with the sweet aroma of Jenna.

He resisted his first urge, which was to lean in and breathe deep.

"Now, I'm going to show you the chord."

She nodded, just a single upward motion of her head.

"Now strum," he instructed.

Awkwardly, she ran her fingers across the strings over the sound hole.

"Wow," she said, strumming again.

"It sounds pretty good!" A moment later, she turned, her mouth curved up into a brilliant smile. About six inches from him. She froze, staring into his eyes, clearly surprised to find him so close.

His heart thundered in his chest and he couldn't for the life of him look away from those beautiful, emerald-shaded eyes of hers.

Books by Lissa Manley

Love Inspired

*Family to the Rescue
*Mistletoe Matchmaker
*Her Small-Town Sheriff
  A Snowglobe Christmas
    "A Family's Christmas Wish"
*Hometown Fireman
  Storybook Romance
*Small-Town Homecoming

*Moonlight Cove

LISSA MANLEY

decided she wanted to be a published author at the ripe old age of twelve. After she read her first romance novel as a teenager, she quickly decided romance was her favorite genre, although she still enjoys digging into a good medical thriller now and then.

When her youngest was still in diapers, Lissa needed a break from strollers and runny noses, so she sat down and started crafting a romance and has been writing ever since. Nine years later, in 2001, she sold her first book, fulfilling her childhood dream. She feels blessed to be able to write what she loves, and intends to be writing until her fingers quit working, or she runs out of heartwarming stories to tell. She's betting the fingers will go first.

Lissa lives in the beautiful city of Portland, Oregon, with her wonderful husband, a grown daughter and college-aged son, and two bossy poodles who rule the house and get away with it. When she's not writing, she enjoys reading, crafting, bargain hunting, cooking and decorating.

Small-Town Homecoming

Lissa Manley

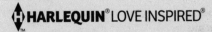

HARLEQUIN® LOVE INSPIRED®

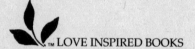

™ LOVE INSPIRED BOOKS

Recycling programs
for this product may
not exist in your area.

ISBN-13: 978-0-373-81777-1

SMALL-TOWN HOMECOMING

www.Harlequin.com

Printed in U.S.A.

Judge not that you be judged. For with that judgment you pronounce, you will be judged, and the measure you give will be the measure you get.
—*Matthew* 7:1–2

This book is dedicated to Shana Asaro. Thank you for all of your hard work on my books. I'll miss you.

Chapter One

Curt Graham pulled Old Green up to the curb in front of the Sweetheart Inn, cut the engine and climbed out of the pickup. He breathed deep, enjoying the familiar salty tang in the ocean air. Given he'd left Moonlight Cove in disgrace ten years ago, it was hard to believe he was back where he'd grown up. Hopefully for good, although he had no illusions about the difficult road he'd chosen by returning.

He paused for a moment and looked up at the puffy clouds scudding across the late-afternoon sky.

Please, Lord, help me to continue in my recovery by making good choices, and give me the strength to face the many mistakes I made in the past.

He stepped forward and opened the iron gate guarding the front yard, casting his gaze over the white Victorian-style home, noting that the place was in need of a new coat of paint and fresh gingerbread window trim. But the house was beautiful, and if he remembered correctly, had been run by an old couple since long before he'd been born.

He closed the gate and headed up the concrete pathway that led to the front steps of the Sweetheart, his gaze lingering on the bright red roses still blooming in the front yard. Summer typically came late to the Washington Coast, if at all, really, and many flowers were still in bloom, even in mid-September.

As he went up the wooden stairs, he saw that a wide front porch wrapped around the front of the house and a gliding rocker sat at an angle in one corner, flanked by two padded outdoor chairs. Red flowers in pots sat clustered by the painted railing. Looked like a good place to relax, although with the temperatures dropping as summer gave way to fall, hanging out on the porch in the evening would be mighty chilly very soon.

Just as Curt hit the top of the stairs, the wide wooden front door flew open and a dark-haired boy of about six, maybe seven, blasted out, full speed ahead. Luckily he saw Curt and deftly dodged him before he trucked down the stairs without missing a step.

A feminine voice rang out from the house. "Sam Waters, come back here this instant!"

Giggling, the boy kept going when he reached the bottom of the stairs and ran around the front corner of the house.

Curt paused by the porch railing and debated going after the kid, but before he could get in gear to do so, the front door banged open again and a pretty young woman with curly red hair came barreling out.

She put on the brakes when she saw Curt, windmilling her arms, and barely managing to stop before she ran fully into him.

"Oh. Sorry. Um…" She cast her gaze around, then looked at him with flashing green eyes. "Did you see where he went?"

"Around the corner," Curt said, pointing in the direction the kid had gone.

"Okay, thanks," she said, bestowing him a crooked smile. "I'll be right back."

He watched her go, admiring her slender curves as she quickly descended the stairs and took off in the direction Sam had gone.

"Sam, don't do this again," she called, her voice ringing with frustration. "Remember we talked about this after yesterday's incident? You promised you wouldn't misbehave today."

Curt stood by the railing, listening, then slowly went down the stairs, curious about what was going on with the boy and the attractive young woman.

Just as he reached the grass, she screamed, "Don't you dare!"

That sounded serious. His protective instincts—and curiosity—surging, Curt took off, rounded the corner of the house and ran into the backyard.

His gaze zeroed in on them, facing off in the far back corner. Sam held the end of a nozzled garden hose in one hand and was pointing the "weapon" toward the young woman, who had one hand out as she inched closer to Sam in a half crouch.

"I mean it, Sam…." she said.

Sam's face was lit by a mischievous smile that, in Curt's opinion as a formerly ill-behaved boy, didn't bode well for her. Nope.

Figuring he could diffuse the situation—somehow—Curt kept moving toward the dueling duo, noting as he did that Sam wasn't fazed in the least, and was moving forward, hose held out in front of him.

Curt turned his attention to her again. She shook a rigid finger at Sam. *"Do. Not. Spray. Me. With. That. Hose."*

"Hey, bud," Curt shouted, waving his arms. "Put down the hose, okay?"

Curt drew alongside the woman. She threw him a grateful look.

"Who're you?" Sam called, one eyebrow raised.

"I'm Curt Graham."

The boy shrugged as if to say, "Big deal, your name means nothing to me."

"I'm checking in here," Curt said by way of an explanation. Maybe he could distract the boy by talking long enough to nab him.

The woman threw him an apologetic look. "Jumping right into the fun stuff, huh?"

"Right."

Out of the corner of his eye, Curt saw Sam moving closer, presumably to strike, up close and personal. Curt turned to face the threat; he could take this kid, no problem. Working out was part of his recovery, so he was fitter than he'd ever been, right? This little kid was no match for him.

Curt held up his hands. "Sam—"

Before he could get any more words out, Sam raised the hose and pointed it directly at the woman's face. Curt was sure he saw the kid's finger tighten on the nozzle trigger.

Instinctively Curt pushed the woman behind him and then he rushed Sam, hoping to catch him and wrest the hose away before he could inflict any liquid damage. Only to be met with an icy-cold blast of hose water right in the kisser.

Jenna Flaherty widened her eyes and squawked as her handsome, dark-haired new guest took a hard spray of water intended for her directly in the face. But the torrent of water didn't seem to deter

Mr. Graham. He just kept moving toward Sam, his arms in front of him, trying to dodge the spray.

Sam shrieked and kept backing up, wildly shooting water as he went, holding the hose with both hands.

She watched in an odd kind of fascination as her rescuer determinedly picked up the pace, putting his long legs to work. Sam's eyes widened and his feet got tangled up in each other, and he stumbled and lost ground, fast. But his finger somehow kept pressing the nozzle trigger and the water kept pummeling Mr. Graham. Jenna had no idea how he wasn't inhaling oodles of water.

With a growl, Mr. Graham lunged at Sam, who dropped the hose as he tried, too late, to escape the much larger, stronger man. Mr. Graham managed to catch Sam around the waist and haul him up against his wide chest.

Sam flailed his legs. "Put me down!" he screamed.

"Not happening," Mr. Graham said, his coffee-colored eyes glinting in the sun. He shook the water out of his face as he hugged Sam against him to keep control of the squirming boy. "No way am I taking more water up my nose."

Mortified, Jenna ran forward. "Sam, stop this nonsense at once!"

Sam had trouble with impulse control—a hallmark symptom of his ADHD—so his behavior didn't surprise her. Especially since she'd been his after-school day-care provider for almost a year, and was well aware of the challenges Sam faced, what with his dad in prison and his mom juggling two jobs to make ends meet.

But the last thing she needed was to lose a client because of Sam's behavior. Business was down at the Sweetheart, and with her bank account depleted by the costly repairs Grams had put off and that were now Jenna's responsibility, she needed every penny of income she could get just to keep the place afloat.

Mr. Graham looked at her over Sam's head, then jerked his chin toward the hose. "You might want to get that thing while you can."

"Oh, yeah." She went over to the hose bib and turned the water off at the source. Picking up the nozzle, she dragged the hose over and put it under a large rhododendron bush, where Sam would have a harder time getting to it.

"Let me go," Sam whined, trying in vain to pry Mr. Graham's well-muscled arm loose from its seemingly iron grip around Sam's waist.

Setting her jaw, she headed in their direction. As she neared, she couldn't help noticing that being blasted by a torrent of water hadn't detracted from Mr. Graham's good looks one bit. His short dark hair stood on end, but with his tall build, lean but muscular physique and matching dark eyes, he was one good-looking guy, indeed.

She shoved that rogue thought aside, her ire at Sam rising again. But she tamped it down, reminding herself that she needed to be firm yet loving with the boy. Sam was going through a rough time and needed levelheaded discipline like nobody's business.

"Mr. Graham will put you down as soon as you calm yourself, Sammy." She looked at Mr. Graham, nodding slightly. "Right?"

He nodded back, clearly getting her drift. "Right. But no more funny stuff, bud. This kind of behavior isn't cool."

Sam quit squirming and went still in Mr. Graham's arms. "Yeah, I guess."

Mr. Graham lowered him to the ground, but kept his hands on the boy's narrow shoulders while he leaned sideways to look him in the eye. "I want a promise that you're going to behave."

"All right, I promise," Sam grudgingly said.

"Good deal." Mr. Graham let go of Sam's shoulders and stepped back as he wiped the water from his face, though he'd probably have to change clothes, Jenna thought. His short-sleeved light blue polo shirt and jeans were soaked.

Sam skittered sideways, out of the man's reach, but otherwise stayed put and kept his promise. For now. She knew better than anyone that Sam had a hard time staying out of trouble.

Relieved that the garden hose crisis had passed,

Jenna stepped forward and extended her hand to Mr. Graham. "Belatedly, I'm Jenna Flaherty, owner of the Sweetheart Inn."

He wiped his hand on his jeans and held it out, engulfing her hand in his large grip. "Yes, we talked last week. Nice to meet you. As I said before, I'm Curt Graham."

"I recognize you," she said, details coming together in her mind.

He cocked his head to the side. "Really?"

"Yes, you used to live in Moonlight Cove, right? I spent summers here at the Sweetheart with my grandmother and grandfather, Jean and Silas Marton." Every teenage girl in town had been aware of the Graham brothers. Though she was a few years younger than Curt, she'd eventually been old enough to appreciate him when she'd seen him in town during the summer. Of course, she'd been much too shy and awkward to ever speak to him.

"I remember your grandparents," Curt said, nodding slowly. "Your grandpa drove a big black Caddy, didn't he?"

"Yes, he did. He loved that car." It had just about killed Jenna to have to sell it to a collector a year ago to pay for a new roof for the inn.

"They ran this place for years, didn't they?"

She nodded. "They started it back in the sixties." They'd put years of hard work and sweat into running the inn. Her chest clutched a bit. "My grandpa died three years ago, and I moved down here to help Grandma with the place." A massive heart attack had killed Gramps instantly. Grams had never really been the same—losing her partner after so many idyllic years of marriage had devastated her.

"Oh, I'm sorry to hear that. How's your grandma doing?"

"Not so well." Jenna sighed shakily. "She has some pretty severe dementia, and I had to move her into a nursing home three months ago." The horrific disease had robbed Grams of the ability to care for herself, and with the inn to run, Jenna had had no choice but to move her to a skilled-care facility.

"Oh, that's rough," Curt said, his eyes soft. "My grandpa died of complications from Alzheimer's."

"So you know how difficult it is." Putting her grandma in a home had been the hardest thing Jenna had ever had to do. "But she's happy there, and gets excellent care. I visit every Sunday." Thankfully, due to Gramps's careful investing, Grams had the money to pay for her care. Unfortunately, she hadn't had the head or the heart for maintaining the inn in the past few years, so that responsibility had fallen to Jenna when Grams had signed over the deed to the inn a little over a year ago.

"I'm sure you did the right thing."

"Thanks." Jenna wasn't so sure, but she was trying to deal with all that had happened, and was determined to make a success of the Sweetheart.

Shifting gears, she moved her gaze to Sam, who stood nearby, fidgeting. She gave him a stern look. "Sam, is there something you need to do?"

Sam blinked, looked around, then glanced down at his wet T-shirt. "Change clothes?"

She crossed her arms over her chest. "How about you apologize to Mr. Graham?"

"Oh, yeah." Sam hunched his shoulders and looked at the grass at Curt's feet. "Sorry I got you wet."

"You need to look him in the eye when you apologize," she reminded Sam. She did her best to instill manners and respect in Sam.

He huffed but complied, looking up—way up— at Curt. "I'm sorry I got you wet."

"Mr. Graham," Jenna reminded.

"Who else would I be talking to?" Sam said.

Jenna held on to her patience with a thin thread. "No, you need to say, 'I'm sorry I got you wet, *Mr. Graham.*'"

Sam rolled his eyes, then stopped himself and looked at Curt again, a smidgen of contrition shining through. "I'm sorry I got you wet, Mr. Graham."

Curt smoothed his damp hair back. "Well, I was

a boy your age once, so I know all about being wild." He smiled at Sam. "And a little water never hurt anyone. But you need to listen to your mom when she talks to you, okay?"

Sam scrunched his face up. "She's not my mom."

Jenna stepped forward. "I take care of Sam after school."

"Ah, I see," Curt said.

"Why don't we go inside, and you two can change and we can get you checked in, Mr. Graham."

"Call me Curt."

"Okay." She gestured to the house. "If you guys want a snack, you can have a slice of— Oh, no! My pies!"

She took off at a run, went up the back stairs and flung open the screen door that led to the kitchen. The second she entered the house, a burning smell drifted her way.

She raced across the kitchen, noting that the oven timer had gone off while she was out on garden hose patrol. Praying she could salvage the desserts, she grabbed an oven mitt off the counter and yanked the oven open. Hot, acrid smoke wafted out.

With a muttered exclamation, she pulled out the rack. The trio of pies sat on the cookie sheet she'd baked them on, only they looked more like blackened lumps of dough than anything remotely edible. She should have known better than to leave the ancient oven unmonitored. The appliance was touchy about maintaining an even temperature, and until she could afford to replace it with a newer, more reliable model, she had to keep a close eye on everything she baked. And a new-model oven would come after a new porch, fresh exterior paint and a new furnace. The list was endless. The money was not.

Sighing, she set the cookie sheet on the stove. She regarded the ruined pastry, shaking her head. She'd followed Grams's dog-eared recipe to a T, and had wanted these to be as sigh-worthy as Grams's pies had always been. Instead, Jenna had ended up with ugly blobs of black dough that were far from the ideal she wanted to uphold.

Her grams's pies always turned out bakery perfect.

She threw the mitt on the counter, then turned and saw Sam and Curt heading into the kitchen, Sam in the lead.

Curt's eyes went to the pies. "Oh, wow." He came over and stood next to her, gazing at the burned mess, his hands on his narrow hips. "Guess you didn't catch them in time."

"Nope," she replied, trying to ignore how his damp hair was drying all wavy and touchable.

"They're ruined. Guess I have some more baking to do."

He furrowed his brow. "They look fine to me. Nicely browned, in fact. That just adds flavor. I'd eat them, no problem."

"You would?"

"Sure," he said, shrugging. "Pie is pie."

She liked his laissez-faire attitude, but too much was at stake for her to share his outlook. "While I appreciate your willingness to eat burned dough, these aren't up to snuff." She sighed.

He regarded her, his long-lashed brown eyes steady.

Her heartbeat skipped and she stepped back automatically.

"Hmm. I know what we have here," he said with a tiny smile.

"You do?" Somehow she was able to make her voice steady when her pulse was going through the roof.

"A perfectionist, perhaps?"

Sam chimed in. "Yeah, Miss Jenna likes everything to be just right." He frowned. "She makes me redo my homework all the time."

"Yes, I'm a real slave driver in the homework department," she said, infusing some dry levity into her voice.

"What's a slave driver?" Sam asked, his nose scrunched up.

"Someone who makes little kids do homework," Jenna explained. She'd majored in education, and knew that if Sam fell behind now because of his focus issues, he might never catch up. Early elementary education set the groundwork for the rest of a child's schooling.

"Sounds like Miss Jenna is just trying to help you out," Curt said. "And that's good for you. School is important."

"Exactly," Jenna said, giving Curt a grateful look. "And sometimes striving for high ideals is necessary." She'd know, being the only unperfect person in a family of perfect people, the one who'd always had to work harder for everything.

"I think Miss Jenna should take all the time she needs to make the pies up to her standards." Curt turned dark eyes her way.

"Thank you. And I need these to be perfect because two of them will be for a wedding reception I'm catering here tomorrow. I have to remake them." She made all of her dough from scratch, so the process wasn't as quick as unrolling premade store-bought crust. "I'll do that later tonight."

"Remember, I have the play at my school tonight," Sam piped in, plopping down in one of the kitchen chairs next to the small table set in one corner. "You promised you'd come."

She arranged her face in a serene expression; she *had* forgotten about the play, not that she'd let Sam know that. "And I never break my promises, so I'll be there." It would be a late night. Unless… She looked at her watch. Still relatively early. "Maybe I could get them done now, before dinner."

"I thought we were going to work on my model car," Sam said, his voice bordering on a whine.

Where was her brain? "Oh, yeah, we were. No problem." She wasn't about to flake out on Sam, not when so many other adults in his life had done so. Even if it meant staying up late to remake her pies. "Go get it out of your backpack, and we'll get right on it."

Curt looked back and forth between them, both brows raised. "Model car?"

"Yeah!" Sam said, jumping from the chair. He puffed out his chest. "I bought it with my own money."

Jenna smiled. Sam had saved for months to buy the model kit.

"Cool, dude," Curt said, nodding. "I built a few models in my day."

Sam's eyes went wide. "You did?"

"You bet. I've always been into cars."

"You wanna help me?" Sam said.

Jenna held out a hand. "Sam, Mr. Graham just arrived. I'm sure he has other things to do."

Curt turned his long-lashed eyes her way.

She forced herself not to stare.

"Actually, I don't start work at the Sports Shack until tomorrow," Curt said. "So after I get changed, I'll have plenty of time to help him."

She blinked, a bit taken aback by his offer. "He just sprayed you in the face with a garden hose."

Curt shrugged one broad shoulder. "No harm, no foul." He scruffed Sam's head. "Besides, he apologized. So no hard feelings."

Wow. What a generous offer. "Well…"

"And if I help him with the model," Curt said, continuing, "you'll have time to get your pies in the oven, and everyone's happy."

"I don't want to impose," she said, holding back out of courtesy, even though letting him take over with the model car project *would* help her out. She had a lot on her plate these days. Actually, her plate was overflowing. But she'd deal. She'd promised Grams she'd keep the inn going, and she would, no matter what.

Besides, Flahertys never failed.

"It isn't an imposition." Curt looked at Sam. "It'll be fun. I haven't built one of those models in years."

"Are you sure?" Jenna asked, touched by his generosity. "Because I can fit the pies in later tonight." She was used to working odd hours.

"I'm sure."

"Please, Miss Jenna," Sam said, bouncing up

and down. "I really want someone who knows what they're doing to help me."

Her resolve frittered away. How could she refuse Sam, especially when she knew he'd craved interaction with adult men ever since his dad had gone to prison? Sam needed a role model, for sure.

Of course, she was assuming a lot about Curt Graham being an appropriate role model, and, obviously, she didn't know him at all. But she knew his brother Seth, and he was a good man. A great man, actually, with a wonderful family of his own. Besides, Sam and Curt would be right here with her the whole time. She could supervise.

"All right, then," she capitulated. "I'll bake while you guys work on the model."

Sam whooped. "Yippee! I'll go get it."

"Hold on, cowboy. You need to go change your clothes first," she reminded the boy. "Do you remember where we put your change of clothes, in the closet down the hall?"

"I remember." Grinning, Sam ran out of the kitchen, then skidded to a halt and turned in the arched doorway that led to the formal dining room and living room. "I'll meet you back here, Mr. Graham, okay?"

Curt saluted. "Okay. See you back here in a few."

Sam took off again, and Jenna heard his footsteps clomping on the hardwood hallway that led to the closet.

She turned her gaze to Curt. "Are you sure about this? You must be tired after driving in from…" Oh. She had no idea where he'd come from.

"L.A., but I overnighted in Portland, so I only drove a couple hours today. And I'm not tired at all. But I am wet," he said, gesturing down to his damp clothes. "I'll go grab my stuff and get changed, and then Sam and I can get busy on his project."

She pressed a hand to her mouth, bemoaning her absent brain again. "Oh, goodness, I'm so sorry. I kept you in here, talking, in wet clothes."

He shook his head, his brown eyes glinting. "No worries. I'm tough."

Yes, she could see that. Tall. Strong-looking. Tough for sure. And handsome with his dark curly hair and café au lait eyes. Something fluttered in her chest and she recognized the feeling for what it was—she was attracted to Curt Graham. No doubt about it.

She cleared her throat, a bit dismayed by her reaction. "Well, thank you for your offer. I really appreciate it, and I'm sure Sam does, too."

Curt pointed toward the front of the house. "Let me go get my luggage. Where should I take it?"

Oh, yes, another detail forgotten. Curt Graham had her flustered, indeed. "I'll meet you at the front door and take you up to the Carnation Room."

"Great," he said, heading out the same archway Sam had gone through. "I'll be right back."

Jenna watched Curt go, appreciating his lean yet broad-shouldered frame and his decidedly masculine, confident way of moving. He definitely was nice to look at. She shook her head and tried to reel her interest in, forcing herself to recall her last relationship during her senior year in college.

Garrett had had the same kind of confidence as Curt, and had been fun-loving and thoughtful, too. She'd gone with her heart 100 percent and had flung herself into a relationship with him. But she'd been wrong in the end about him. And she'd come away with a broken heart and one more reason to believe that she wasn't good enough.

She'd learned then and there that she needed to be cautious in love. Thoughtful. Picky. She wholeheartedly believed in the romantic gold standard she saw in her parents', brother's and grandparents' marriages. She wanted what they had. Desperately.

She headed out to the foyer, reiterating her mantra: *when I fall in love, I will not settle for anything less than a man who will make all my dreams come true.* Curt seemed good at a glance, but only time would tell the story about him she needed to hear.

Until then, she had to keep her interest in him under tight control. And her gaze away from those gorgeous brown eyes of his.

Chapter Two

"So, do you have any kids?"

Curt looked at a bright-eyed Sam perched on the edge of the chair next to him. Man, Sam was a curious little guy. So far he'd asked Curt where he lived, what kind of car he drove and if he had a dog because he, Sam, loved dogs and wanted one of his own—the bigger the better—but his mom wouldn't let him have one because they had a cat instead.

"Nope, no kids." Curt liked children well enough, but having his own seemed unlikely. Maybe way, way down the road. His goal now was to mend fences and put order into his life.

He picked up the bottle of model glue and handed it to Sam. "Now, I'm gonna hold these two pieces, and you're gonna put some glue where they meet, all right?"

"'Kay." Sam took the glue and waited for Curt

to get the two pieces into place. "Why don't you have kids?"

Curt picked up the pieces and held them out, touching. "'Cause I'm not married," he said, going with the easy answer rather than the one that would require any explaining.

Sam cocked his head to the side. "Why not?"

Curt frowned and then looked over at an apron-clad Jenna as she pulled the remade pies out of the oven, noting the delicate curve of her chin, rosy cheeks and the lovely shade of her large green eyes. Boy, she was pretty.

She set the pies on the counter and then shrugged and gave him a lopsided smile, as if to say, "Yeah, he's curious. Deal with it."

"Put the glue right there," Curt said, stalling while he tried to figure out what to say.

Sam bent over and very carefully applied some glue where Curt had indicated, his brow creased. When he was done, he sat back. "So?"

"So, what?" Curt said, very carefully setting the glued pieces down. Maybe Sam would forget the question.

Sam sighed. "So, why aren't you married?"

No such luck. Curt looked back at Jenna with a "rescue me" look. She pressed her lips together, shot him a quick, furtive glance, and then in what seemed like a very deliberate manner, set about running water into the sink without looking his way again. No help there. Was she enjoying seeing him on the spot? Or…waiting for his answer?

"Um…well, I haven't met the right person," Curt said. True enough—the wild crowd he'd hung out with in L.A. hadn't been into much beyond scoring their next hit. Committed relationships had been few and far between. But he wasn't sharing those details with the kid.

"What about Miss Jenna?" Sam asked. "She's not married, either."

Curt raised a brow and looked at Jenna. She was washing a mixing bowl with such intense care it seemed as if it were made of spun glass rather than stainless steel. "Really? Well, then, maybe I'll ask her out."

The bowl fell into the sink with a *clank* and her wide-eyed gaze flew his way. *"What?"*

He just smiled innocently. "Turnabout is fair play."

"What's turbinout?" Sam asked.

Curt leaned back against the ladder-back of his chair. "It's when someone returns what they've been given."

Sam scowled. "Like if I gave a Christmas present back to Santa?"

"Yup, kinda like that," Curt said.

"Oh. That's bad," Sam said. "But what does that have to do with you and Miss Jenna going out on a date?"

Jenna sputtered, glaring at Curt. "Sam, he's just joking. He and I aren't going to go out on a date."

"Oh." Sam's shoulders hunched as he fiddled with the tube of glue. "My mom goes out a lot. Maybe you can go out with her, Mr. Graham."

"Well, thanks, Sam, but I'm not going to have time to go out while I'm here. I'm going to be working for my brother."

"Who's he?" Sam asked.

Curt picked up the model's directions. "His name is Seth and he owns the Sports Shack."

"Oh, yeah. I know him. I went there to get my stuff for baseball." Sam smiled. "He's nice."

"He has a little boy just about your age."

"What's his name?"

"Dylan," Curt said, looking for the car's hood piece.

Sam put the tube of glue down. "Dylan's lucky he has a dad. My dad's in jail, but my mama says he's getting out soon."

Curt's heart lurched and he looked to Jenna. She nodded solemnly.

"Oh, wow, Sam. I'm sorry." Curt knew how rough it could be for a kid to grow up with bad parents. Emotional neglect had been part and parcel of his childhood, and had left profound scars. He wouldn't wish that on anyone.

"Hey, lookee, Mr. Graham," Sam said, holding his fingers up. "I glued my fingers together!"

"What?" Jenna came running. "Let me see."

Sam held up both hands. Curt bent closer to look at the same time Jenna did and they almost bumped heads. Curt backed off a bit, but her flowery-smelling hair hung down in front of him, surrounding him in a soft shampoo cloud.

Sure enough, Sam had glued his two forefingers together. "Er…yep, you sure did," Curt remarked.

"Oh, no, Sam." Jenna put her hands on her hips. "This stuff is permanent."

Sam's eyes went huge.

Curt squeezed his shoulder. "Don't worry, bud. I can unstick them."

"You can?" Jenna asked.

"Sure. Do you have any nail polish remover?" Curt asked Jenna.

"Yes, I do. I'll go get it. Sam, stay put," she said with a pointed finger. She turned and left the room.

"Are you sure you can unstick me?" Sam asked, looking worried that he was going to walk around with his fingers stuck together. "I'm a tree in the play tonight, and I have to be able to wave my arms."

"Don't worry, I'll fix it right up."

Jenna returned, a small bottle in her hand. "Here we go." She handed it to Curt and then went over and got a paper towel. "You sure this will work?"

"I'm sure. I stuck my fingers together all the time when I was a kid, and so did my brothers. We figured out soon enough how to take care of it." He unscrewed the lid of the remover. "A bit of this and you'll be good as new."

It took a few minutes of gentle work, but soon enough Sam's fingers separated. "See?" Curt said. "Unstuck."

"Thanks, Mr. Graham," Sam said, examining his fingers. "That stuff is strong."

"Yeah, it is. My brother Seth and I once glued the toilet seat down with this stuff. My dad had a fit over it, too." Dad had stomped around for days after that prank, and had picked a fight with Mom over the whole thing. Somehow that had turned into a battle of epic proportions, with Dad sleeping on the couch for weeks and Mom sobbing behind closed doors.

That was the way things usually went in the Graham household during Curt's childhood. Fight. Make up. Fight again. Until Curt spent some time in his friends' houses, he'd thought all parents were in a constant war. Turned out it was just his.

That had been a significant turning point in his life. Unfortunately, he'd turned the wrong way.

And now, not surprisingly, his parents were divorced. Mom had done well. Dad? Curt wasn't exactly sure.

"Don't get any ideas," Jenna said to Sam. "This glue is for car models only."

"Right," Curt said, trying to sound stern, hoping he hadn't inadvertently given Sam any ideas. "Models only."

"Yoo-hoo, I'm back," a female voice called.

Curt turned and saw a little gray-haired woman toddling into the kitchen, a huge pink purse slung over her shoulder. She wore a powder blue pantsuit with thick-soled snow-white tennis shoes and sported bright red lipstick on her thin lips.

Curt rose.

"Miss Landry, you're back," Jenna said. "Join us." She pulled out a chair.

As she moved toward the chair, Miss Landry's gaze landed on Curt. "Well, who is this?" She slowly sat in the chair, holding her purse across her body as if it held the crown jewels.

Jenna made the introductions. "Miss Eileen Landry, this is Mr. Curt Graham, our new guest." Jenna regarded Curt. "Miss Landry has been staying with us while she is in town visiting her ill sister."

Curt held out his hand. "Good to meet you, ma'am."

Miss Landry took his hand in her tiny one. "Yes, it is." With shrewd blue eyes she looked him over from her perch on the chair. "My, aren't you a handsome fellow."

Her directness took him by surprise. "Um… thank you."

She turned sharp eyes to Jenna. "I assume you noticed, my dear."

Jenna stilled. "Er, well, of course." She smiled brightly as she went to the stove, seemingly studiously avoiding Curt's gaze. "Can I get you some of that chamomile tea you like so much?"

"That would be wonderful," Miss Landry said. "Then I'm going to go take a little nap before dinner. I wore myself out shopping on Main Street. Of course, the exercise does me good, but I'm old, and I am a bit weary."

"Do you have anything that needs to be brought in?" Curt asked at the mention of shopping. "My mom never returned from shopping without at least one bag."

"Why, yes, I do, actually." She slid a set of keys attached to a stretchy thing off her slender, age-spotted wrist and held them out to Curt. "The bags are in the trunk."

Curt took the keys, then crooked a thumb over his shoulder, looking at Sam. "You want to help me, bud?"

"Yes!" Sam said, springing to his feet. "Can I push the button that opens the trunk?"

"You bet," Curt said.

Miss Landry patted her purse, regarding Sam. "I have some candy in here. You can have a piece when you get back."

"Okay," Sam said, tugging on Curt's elbow. "Let's go!"

He and Sam went out to Miss Landry's car, a huge baby blue boat of a luxury car, circa 1995. He noted that light blue seemed to be a theme with her.

Sam gleefully pushed the button on the fob and the trunk popped open. He and Curt grabbed the bags in the trunk and carried them back into the house, setting them at the base of the oak staircase near the front door.

Curt followed a skipping Sam back into the kitchen.

"Excellent work, young man," Miss Landry said to Sam. "Here's your reward." She handed Sam two snack-size candy bars.

Sam took the candy.

"What do you say, Sam?" Jenna asked.

"Thank you," Sam said dutifully.

"Would you like some, Mr. Graham?" Miss Landry asked.

"I never turn down chocolate."

Miss Landry dug two more pieces of candy out of her cavernous purse and handed them to Curt. "So, Jenna told me you grew up here in Moonlight Cove."

"Yes, that's right," Curt said, leaning a hip against the counter as he unwrapped the candy bar. "I'm here to run the Sports Shack for my brother Seth, while he and his family are in Seattle getting a new store set up."

"It's too bad you couldn't stay at his house." Miss Landry turned to Jenna. "No offense, dear."

"None taken," Jenna said.

"I would have," Curt replied, "but while Seth and his family are gone, they're remodeling the house to add a bedroom for their new baby girl, and to bump out the kitchen, too. With construction going on, it made more sense to stay here."

"Ah, I see," Miss Landry replied, nodding. "So, what took you away from this lovely burg, in the first place?"

Miss Landry's question hit him like a bullet and filled him with dread. Of course, he was going to have to explain things to people. But he couldn't just blurt out the truth. It wasn't as if he could say, "Oh, well, yes, I ran around town as a surly teen, creating trouble, crashed my motorcycle while drunk, and left with my tail between my legs and now I'm back 'cause I'm clean after three tries in rehab and I want to start over."

He settled for part of the truth. "I'm a musician, and I went to L.A. to play in a band." The heady lifestyle of L.A. had called to him. Especially after what happened with Dad.

"Hmm." Miss Landry's eyes sparkled. "A musician. I went steady with a musician once. He played piano." She opened a candy bar. "What do you play, dear?"

"Guitar."

Miss Landry nodded approvingly. "Excellent. An artist. And handsome. And single, I presume?"

Curt could only nod.

"Just as I thought—no ring." Miss Landry slanted a glance at Jenna, who was checking the pies on the counter. "Are you paying attention, Jenna?"

Curt's jaw fell. Miss Landry wasn't wasting any time at trying to get him and Jenna together, was she? He'd have to keep his eye on her. She was sharp and dating wasn't on his to-do list. Staying on the straight and narrow and proving himself capable was.

"Why, Miss Landry, are you matchmaking?" Jenna said without missing a beat.

"Well, maybe just a bit," Miss Landry said with a sheepish smile. "I don't want someone as lovely as you to be alone forever."

"What makes you think I'm going to be alone forever?" Jenna asked, taking the teapot off the stove.

Curt's ears perked up.

"Well," Miss Landry said, "if you don't come

up with a more realistic checklist for the man you want, you're never going to find him."

Curt frowned. Jenna had a man checklist?

"I like to think I can keep my list and still find love eventually," Jenna said, pouring boiling water into the flowered mug she'd set on the counter.

Apparently, she did. Huh.

"We'll see," Miss Landry replied with a quirk of her lips.

Jenna's comment reminded Curt that with his troubled history, he wasn't sure any woman with any kind of checklist would be interested in him. No way. The scars of his past ran deep and would be hard—perhaps impossible—to overlook. And with small-town gossip at work, it wouldn't be long before Jenna knew all about his checkered past—or maybe she already did. His gut clenched at that idea.

Miss Landry turned to Curt. "So, what do you do for a living, aside from working with your brother? Music still?"

He geared himself up for giving his rehearsed answer. "I'm between jobs right now, and I want to eventually go to school to become a therapist." He owed his life to his drug counselor, Marv, and wanted to help others in the same way someday.

"Oh, excellent. Very noble of you," Miss Landry said with a warm look. "There's always a need for compassionate listeners and advisers."

"Well, thank you." Curt figured it was about time he did something worthwhile with his life.

"Do you plan on staying in Moonlight Cove permanently?" Miss Landry asked, surreptitiously handing Sam another candy bar under the table. She winked at the boy. He grinned, showing he was missing his two front teeth.

"I hope to," he said, giving the easy answer. But in a small town like Moonlight Cove, people often didn't forgive and forget. He'd need both and was worried neither was possible. "Seth knew I was looking for something here in town, so he offered me the store job to get me started. My goal is to get a permanent job at my brother's store, and go to community college part-time to work on my psychology degree." He definitely had a lot of hard work ahead of him. He liked to think he was ready for the challenge. Or as ready as he'd ever be.

"And do you have family besides your brother still in town?"

Jenna brought a steaming cup of tea over and set it in front of Miss Landry.

"Thank you, dear," she said to Jenna.

Curt hesitated, not sure how much to share about his dysfunctional family. Old habit, one he was going to need to break. Somehow.

"Forgive me," Miss Landry said before he responded. "I'm way too nosy for my own good."

"No, no problem." He was going to have to get used to fielding questions like this, and to talking about his family; there would be no running from people's interest here. "Yes, my parents are still in town. My younger brother, Ian, lives in San Diego."

"So your family called you back?" Miss Landry asked.

"In a way. Seth and his wife, Kim, visited me in L.A., and I met my niece and nephew for the first time. I realized how much I was missing by being away." That realization had surprised him; it had been a long time since he'd actually longed for the connection of family. Interesting how being clean had cleared his mind and made him want things that had never seemed important before.

"Ah, so you have a young niece and nephew. No wonder you returned," Miss Landry said.

"I'm looking forward to being in their lives." He liked the fact that Dylan and Charlotte viewed him with a clean slate. A small thing, Dylan's and Charlotte's rosy views of him, but he was holding on to it like a lifeline. He desperately wanted to be good Uncle Curt, someone whom his niece and nephew could look up to in the future without the shadow of his bad choices shading their opinion of him.

He wanted that fresh start.

"Excellent. Children are such a blessing, though

I was never fortunate enough to have any." She stirred some sugar into her tea. "So you said your parents are still in town?"

His shoulders tensed. "Yes, they are."

"Well, I'll bet they're thrilled to have you back."

Mom, yes. Dad? Not even close. He thought Curt was a worthless loser, and while that opinion hurt, Curt knew he'd earned the attitude with his bad choices. No doubt about it—he had a hard road ahead proving his dad wrong.

But Curt wasn't going to dump details of his and his dad's dysfunctional relationship on Miss Landry. He barely knew her, and he sure didn't want to shock her, or lower her opinion of him. Though…he had to keep in mind what Marv had drilled into him—that Curt had to own up to his past behavior to move beyond it. He'd have to ease into that approach; his shame still had the upper hand a lot of the time.

So, for now, he simply said, "Well, I haven't connected with them yet, so that remains to be seen." He did his best to sound relaxed when he was anything but. He and his dad hadn't spoken since Curt left town.

"Oh, I'm sure they'll welcome you back with open arms," Miss Landry said with a knowing nod. She patted his hand. "What parents wouldn't?"

Curt's gut pitched. *His* parents wouldn't. Well,

not Dad anyway. Mom had always been more forgiving, and they'd talked weekly for the past few months. Curt only hoped he had the courage to deal with his dad—and the Graham family's problems—while continuing to make good choices that would keep him on the path he'd mapped out.

Apprehension formed a knot in his chest. His resolve would be tested soon enough; he had no place to hide as he'd had in L.A. He was bound to run into Dad sooner rather than later. Curt preferred later. Or never, actually.

There would be no running for cover this time, no distance to soften the harsh reality that hung over the Graham family like a sickening haze. And that fact had him worried more than anything else he'd had to face since he'd OD'd and looked death straight in the eye.

Chapter Three

With nervousness eating away at him, Curt opened the door to the Sports Shack and stepped inside. The bells above clanged as the door swung closed behind him. Instantly, the smell of sporting goods—leather and rubber and something indefinable yet totally distinctive—hit him.

He paused and breathed deep, taking it all in, feeling as if his new life was actually starting. He'd saved himself from his messed-up old life, and he only wanted to see it in his rearview mirror.

Excitement bubbled inside, warring with gut-munching apprehension. This store would be his "home" for the next month—and maybe longer if things worked out the way he wanted.

He focused on the excitement, choosing to savor the moment, which had been so long in coming. There had been times in the past ten years he actually thought he'd die before he ever returned to Moonlight Cove, much less actually set foot in Seth's store. Curt had burned a lot of bridges in his life—demolished them, actually—and this opportunity meant everything.

Seth was counting on Curt. He couldn't screw this up.

Setting his shoulders, he moved forward. "Seth?" he called. "You here?" They'd made plans to meet at 9:00 a.m., before the place officially opened, so Seth could train Curt in the ins and outs of the daily running of the store.

Seth came out of his office at the back. "Bro!" He waved and headed toward Curt.

Curt felt something ease inside of him at the sight of his brother. He and Seth, and Ian, their younger brother, shared a bond not only as brothers but as survivors of the dysfunctional Graham household. Few others understood the scars their childhood had caused.

"It's good to see you!" Seth said, embracing Curt.

Curt hugged his brother back. "You, too," he said, choking up a bit, barely able to get the words out.

Seth let him go and pulled back, his blue eyes piercing. "Hey, now. Are you going all emotional on me?"

"Maybe a bit," Curt said sheepishly. "I'm beginning to appreciate how good it is to have family around to support me." In the past, family had meant trauma, stress and fighting.

"You haven't had that in a long time. It's been a rough road," Seth stated.

"More like jagged." Full of potholes and backsliding and enough excuses to fill a dump truck. "I finally feel like I'm on a smoother path." Not perfect. But better. Rock bottom had had a way of making him appreciate that like never before.

Seth went behind the counter. "I hope so." He gave Curt a solemn look. "I'd like my brother back."

A lump sprouted in Curt's throat. "Me, too." He and his brothers had been close growing up, and Curt had always looked up to Seth, the oldest. "I...need to apologize."

"As part of your recovery?" Seth asked.

"Yes, that." There was so much more, though. "But also because...well, you did your best when we were in high school to keep me on the straight and narrow."

"You were hanging out with a bad crowd, making bad choices, and I was worried. Especially when I found the drugs in your drawer."

Curt flinched. "Not my finest moment." He remembered the day during his junior year of high school that Seth, a senior, had showed him the drugs he'd found and confronted Curt about his wild behavior. Regret burned a hole in his gut. His life had been a series of bad moments. "I know I told you this when you visited L.A., but I have to say I'm sorry again. And that I'm going to stay clean. I want to turn my life around."

A year ago, Curt had ended up in the hospital from an overdose. The E.R. doctor had told him that if he kept abusing drugs, he'd die sooner or later. Probably sooner.

Terrified of dying, Curt had gone directly into an inpatient drug treatment program, and had then moved into a halfway house run by a local church charity. The best life decision he'd made until that point. His life had been littered with bad choices.

Finding God hadn't been one of them. The Lord had saved Curt, and he would never forget that God hadn't judged him. He had forgiven him completely, and now Curt was trying to forgive himself and move on to a better life.

"Look how far you've come," Seth replied, pressing his hand to Curt's shoulder. "I'm proud of you, bro."

Curt's eyes tingled. He couldn't remember anyone ever being proud of him. Certainly not himself. "Don't be, yet. My recovery journey isn't complete. Be proud of me when I prove to you that I'm staying clean." For once he needed to show others he was reliable, in control and sober. He desperately wanted to be a good Christian man, hard worker and the kind of person who put his family first, no matter what. He alone was responsible for that.

A pair of pretty green eyes came to mind. Jenna. Look what she'd accomplished on her own, all for the sake of her grandparents' home, because of her staunch love for them. She was a perfect example of the kind of person he hoped to emulate—

The bells over the door rang.

"Uh-oh," Seth said under his breath but loud enough for Curt to hear. "Brace yourself, bro."

Curt frowned, the bottom of his stomach sliding sideways. He froze, his eyes wide. "Why?"

"Because Dad just walked in, and from the looks of the glower on his face, he's on the warpath."

His shoulders bunching, Curt turned. He steeled himself to see the man he hadn't laid eyes on in more than twelve years. After Curt had rammed his motorcycle into a tree, Dad had come to the hospital to tell him not to bother coming home, seeing as he was now a druggie with a record. Worse yet, by virtue of her dead silence, his mom had agreed. It had been a cruel blow to an eighteen-year-old Curt, and he'd never really been the same since.

Angry and hurt, Curt had done just as his dad had asked. He'd gone to live with a friend until he healed, and then he'd left town, sure news of his accident would spread and everyone in town would be judging him and talking about him. He'd told himself he didn't need his family or Moonlight Cove.

Hitting the lowest point of his life recently changed everything.

Sure enough, his dad stood there in the store entryway, looking tired and bitter. Old, too. He'd gone completely gray and had put on a paunch that stretched his dingy shirt tight over his middle. As usual, he was dressed haphazardly in too-short pants, mangled, mud-spattered tennis shoes that looked as if they'd been made when dinosaurs roamed the earth and a beat-up bright orange fishing vest. His face was tanned to a leathery finish by all his hours spent in the sun—while fishing, Curt presumed, if tradition held true—and deep wrinkles fanned out from his eyes and across his forehead. An oncologist's field day.

"Heard you were back in town," his dad said by way of a greeting. He had his face pressed into a tight scowl. A perpetual scowl, if Curt remembered correctly, usually accompanied by harsh words and follow-up criticism.

Curt inclined his head to the left. "Yes, I got in yesterday." He was determined not to let his dad throw him into a tailspin. Duking it out verbally with Dad wouldn't accomplish anything, and Curt was trying to prove himself a changed man. And that meant approaching Dad with a cool, calm demeanor that wouldn't ruffle his highly ruffable feathers.

Although it might throw his dad to discover Curt wasn't going to be his verbal sparring partner anymore. They'd always had a contentious relationship; Curt had been the son his dad was never happy with. Growing up, disappointment had been Curt's middle name.

His dad came closer, his jaw noticeably tight. "Where are you stayin'?"

"At the Sweetheart Inn."

"He's here getting caught up on details before Kim and I leave for Seattle tomorrow," Seth interjected.

His father shook his head and looked at Seth. "I still think you're crazy for bringing him on. As the guy who started this business, I know this place needs someone responsible."

That fire-tipped arrow hit home with perfect accuracy, zinging a familiar lance of pain through Curt's gut.

"He's been clean for six months, Dad," Seth said.

His dad snorted. "So he says."

Curt saw red tinged with the shadows of his misspent past. "It's true," he forced the words out. "Rehab took."

"How many other times have you relapsed?" Dad asked.

A rock lodged in Curt's throat. "Three."

Dad flung his hands up into the air. "See? It won't last. It never does."

"Maybe you ought to give him a chance," Seth replied quietly. "He's worked really hard to get here, and we're his family. We need to support him in any way we can."

Curt met Seth's gaze and nodded his appreciation.

His dad scoffed and rolled his eyes. "Family didn't mean anything to him when he ran around town, drunk and stupid, getting arrested, treating other people like dirt. He brought shame down on the whole Graham family."

"Did it ever occur to you that I acted out to get your attention?" Curt said in a low, raspy voice. "You and Mom were so busy fighting, you didn't pay any attention to us kids." As soon as the words were out, he regretted saying them. Old habits pushing through again.

"Oh, so now you're blaming me and your mom for your crummy choices?" his father said, his blue eyes blazing. "You never did want to take responsibility for your own behavior, Curt. Never."

Curt felt the old resentment building, a tide of anger that manifested itself as a burning wall inside of him. The urge to lash out was strong—

overwhelming, actually—and Curt opened his mouth to blast his dad with both barrels.

But then he realized that would be something the old Curt would do. He didn't want to be that man anymore. Couldn't be if he wanted to build a new life. So he stuffed the vitriol and remembered what Marv had taught him:

Own your behavior.

You cannot fix what you do not acknowledge.

The only thing you can control is your own reactions.

"You're right, Dad," he said, keeping tight control on his tone. "I do need to take responsibility for my behavior."

His dad pulled in his stubbly chin, frowning, clearly flummoxed by Curt's statement.

Curt went on, "I made bad choices, ones I regret. But I want to change that pattern, and that's why I'm back in Moonlight Cove. I want to be a different man, one who can be counted on, one who my niece and nephew will look up to."

"So we're all just supposed to forgive and forget?" his dad asked, his eyes narrow. "Is that what you're expecting?"

"That's what I was hoping for," Curt replied, hating the hesitation in his voice. He'd always felt unsure around his father and it looked as if that emotional reaction hadn't changed. His heart sank. Another daunting challenge to face and deal with. There were so many pieces to be put together in the puzzle of his new life that he could barely keep track of them.

"You always did wish for the moon." His dad shook his head. "All those dreams of being a musician, when you could have just been content to work at the store."

"That was your dream, Dad, not mine," Curt replied. This was an old bone between them—his dad had wanted Curt and his brothers to work in the store, expecting that one of them would someday take over. They'd had this argument in so many ways over the years Curt had lost count.

"Yeah, you've told me that before." His dad ran a hand through his hair, leaving it sticking on end. "You didn't want anything to do with the Sports Shack, and what did you do with your life instead? Wasted it on drugs."

Seth stepped into the fray. "Hey, now—"

Curt held up a rigid hand. "No, I've got this." While he appreciated Seth speaking up on his behalf, Curt had learned that he needed to fight his own battles—without drugs to numb him or give him false bravado.

Seth deferred and stepped back, allowing Curt a moment to rein in his temper. Getting angry would only fuel the fire. And prove to his father that he, Curt, was still a hothead. No matter what his dad threw out, Curt had to stay in control of his emotions, even though his gut was churning and he could feel his pulse beating in his head.

"You're right, I did waste my life on drugs. You think I don't know that?" He took a deep breath. "But now I'm looking for a fresh start, and I've taken the steps necessary to make that happen."

"Fresh start?" His dad gave a derisive laugh. "There is no such thing as a fresh start in life, or I would have made one years ago."

Yeah, Dad had never been able to rise above his hardscrabble childhood as an orphan. In fact, he seemed bent on perpetuating the negative cycle of his youth. Or maybe he just didn't know how to break the circle.

"That's your perspective, and you're entitled to it," Curt said. "But I have a new view on life, new goals, and I'll do whatever necessary to achieve them. I have hope that people will see that I've changed."

His dad snorted, then shook his head. "I'm afraid you'll have to keep on hoping. I'm not going to let you off the hook, and nobody else in this town is, either. The sooner you realize that, the better."

Curt's shoulders went heavy. He did his best not to give in to the downward pull, and tried to stand tall. But after so much time spent crawling through life, remaining upright and strong was hard. Especially when he had his dad shoving him down. But no one had said returning to Moonlight Cove would be easy. "You're entitled to your opinion. I only have control over my own actions, so that's the way I'm rolling."

"Good luck with that," his dad said, giving a mock salute. "You're gonna need it." He turned his attention to Seth, dismissing Curt as if he were a fly on the wall. "Did you get that fishing gear I ordered?"

Seth gave Curt a half-apologetic, half-questioning look, as if to ask if Curt wanted him to intervene.

Curt shook his head ever so slightly. No. He appreciated his brother's willingness to defend him, but nothing Seth could say to Dad would make any difference.

Seth frowned, but then turned his attention to his dad. "Yeah, I did. It's in my office." He gestured sharply to the far wall. "Follow me."

Without a glance toward Curt, his father trailed Seth to the back, leaving Curt alone. With a heavy sigh he leaned his arms on the front counter and put his head in his hands. Dad's attitude stung. A lot. He had zero faith in Curt, and had made it clear he wasn't going to overlook what Curt had done in the past.

Though Curt hadn't really expected anything resembling true forgiveness, he'd nurtured a kernel of optimism that Dad had softened his stance

in the past ten years. And that perhaps the towns-
people would be able to forgive Curt's past sins.
His dad didn't think that was ever happening.

Maybe Curt had hoped for too much. He'd torn
a path of destruction through town during his teen
years and the damage couldn't be repaired. Maybe
he'd always be a pariah: the middle Graham boy
who'd barely made it through high school, caused
trouble, and had almost killed himself one night
twelve years ago while driving drunk.

Suddenly a vision of Jenna rose in his mind's
eye. What would she say if she found out the truth
about him, assuming she didn't know already?
Would she look at him with derision in her eyes,
ticking off his faults one by one as she went down
her perfect-man checklist?

Probably.

A crater formed in his belly.

Another quandary circled around his brain like
a poisonous snake. Had coming back to Moonlight Cove been one giant mistake that would be
more easily left behind than dealt with?

Right now, he was very afraid all of the above
was true and that starting over in Moonlight
Cove—and hoping for love someday—was an
unattainable dream that would never come true.
No matter how hard he tried.

Chapter Four

❧

Wincing, Jenna moved a rented chair into place on the patio and then slowly straightened, stretching her aching lower back. She'd been on her feet since dawn, and had been bending, lifting and carrying in preparation for Phoebe Sellers and Carson Winters's wedding reception in a few hours. Jenna was exhausted.

But she had an event to cater—a paying proposition—which was a good thing all around, and could help generate more event business if the bride and groom were pleased and spread the word. That would be gold in a small town like Moonlight Cove.

So she wouldn't complain—at least not out loud. Besides, her aches and pains were nothing a few aspirin and a hot bath wouldn't help. Later. Much later. She still had a long, busy day ahead of her and probably wouldn't even be finished cleaning up until almost midnight.

Thankfully, the weather had cooperated and they'd be able to go with plan A and have the main part of the reception outside, a risky proposition for the Washington Coast. Phoebe would be thrilled.

Jenna glanced at her watch. Just after noon. The reception started at four o'clock. And she still had tons to do—final food prep, making the flower arrangements, setting the tables. Finishing on time would be close, but she'd make it. She had to. No matter how tired and achy she felt. No one in the Flaherty family relaxed until all of the work was done.

"Hey, looks like you could use some help."

Her heart gave a little blip. She turned and saw Curt stepping onto the patio. He'd left this morning saying he had a meeting with Seth at the Sports Shack, and hadn't been back until now.

"You're a guest." She adjusted the chair's position. "You don't have to help."

He grabbed one of the chairs and put it next to one of the round, tablecloth-covered tables she'd set up. "Things would go a lot faster this way, and you might be able to rest your back if I help some."

She looked at him sideways. "How did you know my back hurts?"

"As someone who's had back problems, I homed right in." He demonstrated, cringing and then stretching. "Hallmark move for an achy spine."

His perceptiveness threw her a bit. He was very observant, and that, for some reason, made her a bit uneasy. She recovered and cocked her head to the side. "You don't look like you have back problems."

"Looks are deceiving," he said cryptically. "I injured my back in a motorcycle accident twelve years ago, and it periodically acts up."

"Wow. Motorcycle accident?" She smoothed out a wrinkle on one of the cloths. "That sounds pretty serious."

"It was. I broke a vertebra and wonked up my spine pretty good, and broke some ribs and my leg." He looked away, but not before she saw a glimpse of a shadow in his eyes. "Spent almost a week in the hospital."

Her hands stilled on the table as horror stabbed through her. "Oh, no. That sounds awful."

"It was," he said quietly. "I left town soon after." Again, she sensed distinct sorrow simmering beneath his surface, a thread of angst that pulled at her.

"Why?" she asked, giving in to her curiosity. "I mean, I would think you'd want to be near your family after such a traumatic event."

He paused with a chair in his hand. "You'd think so. But my family isn't like most families, and…well, my dad and I had a falling-out after the accident, and I decided I needed to leave Moonlight Cove."

Sympathy tightened her heart. "Oh, that must have been a hard decision."

"Yes, it was difficult," he said with thin lips.

She sensed more to the story, but she didn't want to pry. He was a guest, after all, and if he wasn't sharing, there had to be a reason. "You've recovered, I take it, except for your back?"

"For the most part," he said in a tone that, again, made her think he wasn't giving her all the details. Not that he should. They hardly knew each other. "So, you want me to just put the chairs around the tables?"

"You really don't have to help."

"I appreciate your concern, but my back is fine most of the time now, as long as I keep active. And this is my last day until I start working, so you might as well take advantage and put me to work."

She chewed on her lip. Point taken. And, really, at this stage, another pair of hands would be a blessing. "Are you sure you don't mind?"

"I wouldn't offer if I did." He looked at the chairs stacked by the deck railing. "I'll unload all of those and you can go do something else."

"Deal." She gave him a grateful look. "And thanks."

"You're welcome." He went to the chairs. "Oh, how's Miss Landry?"

She hadn't been at breakfast this morning.

Jenna straightened an already straight sapphire-blue tablecloth. "She still has a headache, so she's spending the day in her room."

"Do you think I should go check on her?" He pointed toward the house.

"No, I just did, and she's comfortably reading a gossip magazine." Jenna stood back to make sure the tablecloth was hanging evenly. "She loves those things, the trashier the better."

"Why does that not surprise me?" he asked, grabbing another chair. "She's quite a character."

"She was thrilled when I gave her a magazine stash a past guest had left."

"I only hope I'm half as with it as she is when I get old." He put the chair in its spot.

"Amen," Jenna said. "I've seen what age can do to a person."

"Your grandma?"

She nodded. "Yes. She was a real go-getter in her younger days, and after Gramps died, she just seemed to wither away."

"Broken heart?" Curt asked softly.

Jenna's own heart gave a little shudder; lost love hurt. "Probably." She went over to get another chair from the stack. "They were inseparable and had a perfect marriage. I think she gave up in a way, after he died."

"Here, I'll do that," he said, grabbing the chair she was going for. "Give your back a break."

In answer, a sharp twinge zinged up her spine. She twitched, grimacing, and then rounded her back, trying to ease the ache there. She'd really overdone it. "Okay, okay, you're right, my back is mad. I'll let you do that for me." It was actually nice to have help, a treat for the day, given she usually had to do all the work herself.

He shooed her away. "Go do something else, and when I'm done here, you can put me to work with other chores."

She capitulated, "Okay, I'm going to go arrange the flowers."

Turning, she headed into the house, and then went to the attached garage, where she'd stashed the flowers she'd picked up at the local florist, Penelope's Posies. Meg Douglas, the owner and daughter of Penelope Douglas, the woman who'd originally started the store, had kindly agreed to order the flowers for Jenna at a heavy discount.

The yellow mums, stephanotis, white carnations, dark blue irises and ivy had filled the garage with the wonderful fresh scent of flowers. Jenna inhaled deeply, loving the aroma. She'd always been fascinated with flowers, and if she hadn't ended up as owner and proprietor of the Sweetheart, or a teacher, she'd have become a floral designer. Or maybe a personal chef. Creating things had always appealed to her. She was definitely the only right-brainer in the family; Mom, Dad and her brother, Scott, were much more left-brained.

She went to work on Gramps's old workbench, which ran the length of two sides of the two-car garage. She'd been up late last night setting out the lovely cut-glass vases Phoebe's mom, Grace, had culled from her extensive collection of crystal to be used for the reception.

With necessary efficiency, Jenna went about cutting the flowers and greens to the appropriate lengths. Then, she did her favorite part—arranging the flowers in the containers she'd filled with water earlier. She hummed under her breath as she worked, determined to enjoy the peace and quiet while she had the chance.

As she worked, her thoughts drifted to Curt. He'd been through a lot, and she sensed an untold sad story that beckoned her in a way she didn't quite understand. She knew he'd moved away because of a falling-out with his dad, but what had he done in L.A. for twelve years? Why wasn't an attractive, nice guy like him married?

That question brought her up short. What was it about him that sucked her in and made her want to know everything about him? Well, besides his good looks and the intriguing shadows of his past she saw in his eyes—

"I finished the chairs."

Squawking, Jenna jumped, almost knocking

over one of the vases. She reached out to steady the teetering vase. "Oh, goodness, you scared me!" she said, her heart pounding.

"Sorry, I didn't think I was sneaking up on you," Curt said, moving around the front end of her car.

She put the greenery she'd been working with down. "You weren't. I was just lost in thought." *About you.*

He moved his gaze over her flower-making supplies. "Wow, you've got quite the little florist operation out here."

"Yep, this is where the magic happens." She determinedly directed her attention back to the arrangement she was working on, sliding some ivy into it with shaking hands.

"I didn't realize you were doing so much for the reception. Flowers, food, all the details."

"I offer a menu of items that clients can choose from, and Phoebe liked my ideas so much she opted to have me do just about everything for the reception." Jenna liked to provide as much as possible because it was more lucrative to her bottom line, and lately, with the inn needing so many repairs, the bottom line was important.

"I really don't know how you do all of it." He shook his head. "You make me feel very lazy."

"Trust me, lazy isn't bad. I'd like a lazy day and I don't see one on my schedule anytime soon."

"Why don't you have any help running this place?"

"I can't afford help." She clipped a flower. "I toyed with the idea of hiring someone to do the cleaning—what a relief that would be—but I haven't been able to find the extra money in the monthly budget." Besides, she needed to do this on her own; Mom would be able to run this place with one hand tied behind her back. Jenna had to do the same.

He frowned and came closer. "Is business that bad?"

"Not exactly." She cut the stem off a carnation, trying to keep her eyes on the bouquet. "Business is so-so. But the inn has required a lot of expensive maintenance lately, and the repairs I've had to do have drained my funds in a major way."

"So you own this place?"

"Yeah, Grams signed over the deed to me a year ago." She gave him a little grin. "I was thrilled."

"Have you always wanted a career running a hotel?"

"No, I went to school to become a teacher." She tilted her head sideways and looked at her handiwork. "I had dyslexia as a kid, and always wanted to help kids with learning problems."

"Oh. Wow." He put his hands in his pockets. "And yet here you are, running an inn."

"Well, I spent summers here growing up, and I always loved the place. It was more like a second home than an inn."

"Why is that?"

"Well, mainly because I was out of the shadow of my brother, Scott." She sighed. "He never met an A he couldn't achieve, a sport he couldn't master or an award he couldn't win." Mom and Dad had always been the same way. Overachievers one and all. Jenna had high standards to live up to.

"Ah, one of those."

"Uh-huh." She fluffed the bouquet. "So, when Gramps died, Grams had a hard time running the place on her own, and I hadn't been able to get a teaching job since graduating from college, so I came here to help her."

"Did you know then that the place needed so much work?"

"No, not really. I mean, I knew it was hard work—I saw my grandparents run it for years. But I didn't have a clue to the precarious position the business was in."

"Would that have changed your mind?"

"No," she said. "Keeping the business in the family was just the right thing to do. And I couldn't imagine turning it over to strangers.

Some of my happiest memories took place here, in this house."

He cast his gaze around. "When was the house built?"

"It was constructed in 1928. Grams and Gramps bought it in 1960 and totally refurbished it themselves."

"It has to be expensive to maintain."

"It is. Especially since Grams didn't have the head or the heart to maintain it properly after Gramps's death." It had made Jenna so sad to see Grams give up on life once she was alone. Though in a way, Grams's fading after Gramps passed was a testament to their extraordinary relationship.

"And you never considered selling it?" Curt asked, leaning a hip against the workbench. "From a business standpoint, it might make more sense to get out from underneath the burden of keeping this place going."

She shook her head. "I promised Grams I wouldn't. I'll never forget the day she realized the truth of her own health situation." Jenna swallowed the lump forming in her throat. "She took my hand and begged me to keep the inn afloat, no matter what. How could I say no?" Her dad had pushed for Jenna to take over, too. Jenna could hardly refuse him.

"And…you're the kind of person who never breaks a promise, right?" he said softly.

She liked that he saw that in her; she strived to be dependable and steady. She'd never won an academic award or scored the winning goal in a soccer game, but she could be counted on in tough times. "I try to be." She tilted her head to the side and regarded the bouquet in front of her. Needed more mums.

He looked at the bouquet. "It looks great. In fact," he said, scanning all of her creations, "they all look great."

His praise warmed her up inside. "Thanks."

"What else can I do?" He fidgeted. "I'd rather stay busy."

"Well…they all still need bows." She grabbed the spool of sapphire-blue ribbon Phoebe had picked out. "Wanna help?" Another set of hands was a luxury she should take advantage of while she had the chance.

"Ah, so you're a risk taker, too."

She drew her eyebrows together. "How so?"

"I have no idea how to tie a bow, so you're taking a big risk asking me to help."

"Ah." She saw where this was going. "Well, I know how and it's easy. I'll show you."

"I'll give it my best shot," he said with a rueful smile. "Hopefully you won't regret it. I've never been really crafty."

"Are you underestimating my skills as a

teacher?" she asked in mock seriousness, dropping her chin.

He held up his hands. "No, ma'am. I wouldn't dream of it."

"Good," she said. "Let me tie one so you can see the general method, and then you can try, all right?"

"Sounds like a plan," he replied. "Tie away."

Explaining as she went, she unwound some ribbon and then set out to make a multilooped florist bow, going slower than normal so he could see how it was done. Loop, twist, loop, twist, until she had a pretty bow. Then she attached a pick with wire and put the whole ribbon concoction into one of the floral-filled vases, positioned just so, with the tails of the ribbon trailing down the front of the vase.

"Ta-da!" she said with a flourish. "A lovely bow to grace a lovely bouquet to grace a lovely reception table."

He regarded her with doubt in his eyes. "You actually think I can do this?"

"You can do anything you set your mind to." Words to live by in Jenna's family.

"I'd like to believe that."

She handed him the ribbon. "Don't worry. I'll help with the first one."

"Okay. I'll give it a shot." His shadowed jaw

set with determination, Curt took the ribbon and started looping and twisting as she'd showed him.

After a few tries, he sighed. "This ribbon is slippery," he said after he'd started over twice. "I can't hold on and twist at the same time."

She moved closer, so she was almost touching his elbow. "Put your hand like this," she said, taking a hold of his left hand to adjust the angle. Instantly, tingles traveled from where their hands met up to her arm, and straight to her stomach. A whiff of his spicy aftershave hit her in a wave, all masculine and fresh-smelling. Her breathing went all funny.

"Oh, okay," he said, adjusting his grip on the bow.

Trembling, she let go and moved back, needing space. "So make your loop and twist…"

His brow furrowed, he did as she instructed, but after two twists, the whole thing fell apart. "Oh, man, this is harder than it looks."

"It just takes a little practice," she replied. "Here, let me show you again." She took the ribbon from him, being careful not to make contact with his hand. She had to maintain control.

"You know, maybe I should do something that doesn't have a learning curve," Curt said with a crook of his lips. "I have plenty of time before I have to get ready for the wedding."

"You were invited?"

"Yeah, as the younger brother of the best friend of the bride's brother—otherwise known as the best man—I got an invite."

She blinked. "Huh?"

"Carson and Phoebe are the bride and groom, right?" he explained.

"Right."

"My brother Seth is best friends with Drew Sellers, who is Phoebe's brother and Carson's best man."

Jenna paused. "Ah, okay, I see the relationship now." Everybody seemed to know everybody in Moonlight Cove. Unfortunately, Jenna hadn't had the time for any socializing apart from going to church every Sunday.

"We all grew up together, and I actually had a secret crush on Phoebe for a while."

"Really?" Jenna said, her eyebrows hoisted up.

"Oh, yeah. I wanted to marry her in the worst way."

Jenna's jaw fell. "No way." She'd had no idea that he and Phoebe had dated.

He laughed. "Relax. I was ten at the time."

"Oh." Her face heated. "I thought you meant… well, you know, that you were—"

"In love with her as an adult?"

She nodded.

"No, I was just a kid, and she had these really

cool pigtails and she played a mean game of wall ball on the playground, that's all."

"Got it," Jenna said, relieved for some reason. Although, why should it matter? "I was in love with Jimmy Patton, and all of us girls used to run around and try to kiss the boys."

"Did you catch any?"

"No, all the boys thought we had cooties."

"Obviously this wasn't in high school."

"Nope, third grade. By the time high school rolled around, Jimmy Patton had become James, and he was the star player on the football team." She picked up a white flower and added it to one of the bouquets. "He didn't even know I existed."

"I find that hard to believe."

Jenna's tummy dipped. *You do?* She turned wide eyes to him. "It's true. I was a geek with frizzy hair, freckles and braces, and he was a good-looking athlete with his pick of girls, most of whom were always more put together and with it than I ever was." She shook her head. "I didn't stand a chance. I felt like I went through high school with the word *CLUELESS* tattooed on my forehead."

"That's the thing about high school. It's all about looks rather than what really matters."

"But nobody realizes that at the time, do they?"

"Nope," he said. "They don't. And look at you now. The frizzy hair and braces are gone."

"But, unfortunately, I still have the freckles."

"I like your freckles," he said.

Another *you do?* echoed through her mind, but she held back voicing the words and held her breath instead.

He cast his gaze around, looking suddenly ill at ease, as if he'd said something he shouldn't have. "Um…is there something that I can help you with that requires no skill of any kind? Something that calls for muscles instead of brains?"

She did her best not to look at said muscles, noting his subject change. Probably a good move. She still had a lot to do for the reception, and she really shouldn't be standing around talking about what a nerd she'd been in high school. Nor should she be hoping Curt would compliment her again. Compliments were just words easily thrown out; after Garrett, she put more stock in actions.

"I'm sure we can find something," she replied in a businesslike manner. "Why don't you let me finish up here, and then I'll come in and see what else needs to be done."

"You want me to carry the finished bouquets into the house?"

"That'd be great," she replied, turning her attention back to the unmade bow. "Just put them on the dining room table, and then we can distribute them from there."

"Will do," he said. "I'll wait for that one you're working on and take both of them in at the same time."

"Okay." She started looping and twisting, but her hands were still shaking from his nearness, and she could barely hold on to the ribbon.

"Having some trouble there?" he asked over his shoulder.

She sighed. "I seem to be all thumbs right now." Because of him. "Let's go in and I'll come back to the bows in a few."

"All right, you're the boss." He picked up the finished bouquet and headed into the house.

She hung back for a second, letting out a trembling sigh, striving for balance. Curt was attractive, and seemed considerate and nice. Yeah, well, so had Garrett, and look how that had ended. She hadn't been careful with him, had just jumped into a relationship without thinking. And she'd been clobbered in the end.

She'd trusted her gut with Garrett, and he'd turned out to be jerk. Who knew what kind of man Curt really was? Appearances could be deceiving.

She had to be careful with Curt. Cautious. No matter how appealing he appeared to be.

Chapter Five

Curt pulled on the collar of his shirt, feeling as if he had a noose around his neck rather than a tie. He couldn't remember the last time he'd worn a suit, and it was lucky he could still wear the only one he owned, purchased seven years ago for the imaginary job he'd never quite managed to acquire after a failed stint in rehab.

Looking back on the past ten years of his life made him cringe.

Having been one of the first guests to arrive at the reception, he stood alone on the patio and scanned the space, taking in the beautiful job Jenna had done decorating for the reception. The flowers, placed atop round tables, looked great. On his way in, he'd seen the spread she'd set up in the dining room, and it all looked delicious.

He marveled at all of the balls she had managed to keep in the air today. Food. Decorations. Flowers. She was a one-woman dynamo who managed to be gracious yet focused under pressure. Something he'd never seemed to be able to manage without drinking or taking pills.

She was what he wanted to be—a respected hard worker, focused on tangible goals.

He'd need to watch and learn.

Not that observing Jenna was a chore....

He tugged on his collar again, wishing he could actually relax and enjoy Phoebe and Carson's reception. Honestly, attending felt like too much too fast; he'd already had to deal with his dad completely ignoring him at the wedding, not to mention the stares and what seemed like whispers from the other wedding-goers. Just as he'd imagined, people still remembered him and the things he'd done.

Well, that was the bed he'd made, and he had to lie in it. For once, he was determined to do so without the crutch of drugs.

Things were different now, by his own choosing and his own hard work over the past year. He couldn't give up. No matter how much he dreaded facing his first social event since returning home. Nobody had said his plan would be easy.

He closed his eyes for a moment, sending a prayer up. *Give me strength, Lord, and never let me lose sight of what's important.*

His prayer had his conversation with Jenna running through his mind. He'd spoken the truth in the garage earlier today; he had had a hard time believing she was ever the nerdy girl she'd said she was. She was pretty as all get out now with her pale complexion, striking red hair, green eyes and adorable freckles.

But he'd been one of those guys in high school who'd always gone after the beautiful girls rather than the nice ones, partly because most of the nice ones wouldn't have looked twice at a guy with his reputation. Too bad he'd focused on all the wrong things back then. He wouldn't be making that mistake again. He'd finally grown up and seen what was important. Family. Goals. Being sober.

He heard voices, and within a moment, a group of people dressed in wedding finery stepped out onto the patio. The group included Drew's brand-new fiancée, Ally; Molly Roderick, Phoebe's best friend and matron of honor; and Kim, Seth's wife. Drew, Grant Roderick, Molly's husband, and Seth preceded the ladies outside. Curt hadn't seen Drew for years, and aside from filling out some, he looked pretty much the same as Curt remembered him.

Curt caught Drew's eye and Drew's face lit up. "Curt, my man," he said, coming over and slapping Curt on the shoulder before he held out his hand. "It's good to see you." Drew wore a pearl-gray tux and black bow tie and cummerbund.

Curt shook his hand. "You, too." Drew's warm welcome eased a bit of Curt's apprehension but didn't erase it completely. He was sure there would be others, besides Dad, who wouldn't be so happy to see him back in Moonlight Cove.

"I was so happy to hear from Seth that you were back in town," Drew said.

"Yeah, I figured it was about time to come back and redeem myself."

"Hey, we all make mistakes when we're young."

"You didn't," Curt pointed out.

"Yeah, well, I was boring."

"Not boring. You just had your head screwed on straight." Unlike Curt. "Hey, I hear you're engaged." Seth had filled Curt in on the details of Drew's life this morning.

"Just popped the question last week." Drew tossed a lovesick gaze toward Ally, a pretty, slender gal who had long blond hair. His mouth curved into a goofy grin. "Luckily she said yes."

"When's the wedding?"

"Next spring, most likely. You think you'll still be here?"

"That's the plan," Curt said. "I hear you have a new job, at the fire station in Pacific Beach." Pacific Beach was a small seaside town about a twenty-minute drive up the coast.

"That's right," Drew said, his face glowing with happy pride.

"You always did want to be a firefighter. When we played as kids, you'd always want to pretend that our fort was burning down."

"We had that fort down by the beach." Drew's eyes shined as he reminisced. "Seth, you, Ian and I used to spend hours down there. I think we even tried to convince our parents to let us spend the night there. Mine would never let me."

"Actually, Seth, Ian and I sneaked out several times and camped in the fort."

"Oh, I never knew that," Drew replied.

"We were sworn to secrecy."

"Did your parents ever find out?"

Curt shook his head. "Not that I know of." Mom and Dad had been so immersed in their own problems, they'd never been the wiser.

"You lucked out, then."

Not so much. Though sleeping in the fort had been fun and adventurous, Curt had always wished his parents had taken the time to actually know what was going on with their kids, like Drew's parents had with Drew and Phoebe.

But Curt understood the sentiment behind Drew's statement. And Curt certainly wasn't going to whine about his neglected childhood to Drew. This was supposed to be a happy occasion not a complaintfest. "Yeah, we did a lot of stuff they were never aware of." Easy as pie. Sad as all get out.

Just then, Ally came over and put her arm around Drew. Drew pulled her close against his side. "Hey, honey." He smiled down at her with such love and devotion it made Curt's chest tight. Hoping for a love of his own, along with a new life, just seemed like more than he deserved.

"Hey," she said, returning Drew's smile with a healthy dose of adoration of her own.

Drew made the introductions. "Ally, I'd like you to meet Curt, Seth's younger brother. Curt, this is my fiancée, Ally York."

Curt extended his hand. "Pleased to meet you."

Her green eyes sparkling, she shook his hand. "It's mutual. I hear you just returned to town yesterday."

"That's right."

"Is it good to be home?" she asked.

That remained to be seen. "Yes, it is," he said, going with the requisite answer; no sense in digging up his sordid past if he didn't have to. Besides, he figured she already knew about his history since Drew was fully aware of it.

Ally said something to Drew, and as she spoke, Curt saw more people come out onto the patio, including an older woman and gentleman who looked vaguely familiar. The rail-thin woman wore an ugly short-sleeved dress covered in pink and blue flowers. She had her graying hair pulled up into a tight bun atop her head.

He focused his attention on the woman, trying to figure out who she was. She turned then, too, and locked gazes with him. Her dark eyes narrowed, her jaw dropped and her face twisted into a fierce frown that emphasized every wrinkle on her face.

Without missing a beat, she snapped herself to attention, turned on her heel and headed his way, her back ramrod straight, her steps sharp, all the while staring daggers his way.

"Curt?" she exclaimed, her voice tight. Derisive. "Curt Graham?" She kept coming at him, raising her hand, her finger pointed at him like a knife.

A hush spread over the gathering.

His stomach nose-dived as he finally recognized her. With recognition, a lump formed in his throat, rendering him unable to speak. This wasn't gonna be good.

Within seconds, she was by his side, her roiling bitterness a palpable force to be reckoned with.

He braced himself.

She looked him up and down, her mouth curled into a sneer. "After what you did to my daughter when you dated her, after the path of destruction you caused that awful summer, I can't believe you had the nerve to show your face again in Moonlight Cove." She practically spat the words at him.

Words failed him. Probably because this was his worst imagining coming true, the very reason he'd never come back to town before. People didn't forgive and forget.

All he could squeak out was "Mrs. Woolsey."

Her husband—Mel? Mason?—hurried over, his hound-dog face awash with what looked like a combination of concern and embarrassment. "Now, now, Liz, let's not make a scene," he said, taking her elbow.

Mrs. Woolsey jerked her arm from her husband's grasp. "I'm not making a scene. *He* is, by being here, among upstanding citizens of this good town."

Curt swallowed as her words hit home, battering every promise he'd made to himself to deal with whatever necessary in order to build his new life. "I…I'm sorry you feel that way, Mrs. Woolsey. But that was a long time ago—"

"And that makes your deplorable behavior acceptable?" she asked, her voice rising.

"I'm sorry for the way I treated Amanda, and I'm trying to make amends—"

"Amends?" she scoffed. "Nothing you can say will make your treatment of Amanda all right. You cheated on her, strung her along, treated her like a doormat, exposed her to bad influences."

Seth appeared from inside the house and came to Curt's side. "Mrs. Woolsey, this isn't the place for this discussion."

She drew herself up. "You're right. Anyplace

this man is—" she jabbed a rigid finger toward Curt "—isn't where I want to be."

Her contempt slashed open a raw place in Curt that he'd thought was at least partially healed. He fell back a bit, unable to respond in the face of her scorn.

"Hey, now," Seth said, his jaw noticeably tight. "This is my brother you're talking about."

"Well, I feel sorry for you, then." Mrs. Woolsey stiffly turned to her husband. "We're leaving, Martin." She sniffed, her nose so high Curt was surprised she could see where she was going. "Suddenly the air seems polluted around here."

Mr. Woolsey bobbed his head. "Whatever you say, dear."

She turned her razor-sharp gaze back to Curt. "I will never forget what you did to Amanda, and I'm sure there are plenty of other people in town who feel the same way. If you ask me, you should just turn around and go back to wherever you came from."

Seth stepped forward, but Curt reached out a hand and held him back. While he appreciated Seth's defense, Curt needed to fight his own battles. But not here and now. The last thing he wanted was to ruin Phoebe and Carson's day.

With a contemptuous glare, Mrs. Woolsey stomped off, her milquetoast husband scurrying after her.

Curt's throat thickened as he watched them walk away and he wished the ground would just open up and swallow him whole. Then his gaze snagged on the man hovering in the far corner of the patio next to a potted plant.

Dad. Standing nearby but not defending his son. Agreeing with Mrs. Woolsey by virtue of his silence.

Suddenly, the wound Mrs. Woolsey had ripped open went even deeper. So deep that it reached right into Curt's gut and slashed a big, gaping hole.

As he processed that awful realization, he spied Jenna at the door, a tray in her hands, watching him, her eyes wide. Obviously, she'd witnessed the whole confrontation. If she hadn't known anything about his grimy history here in town, she sure did now.

Curt's humiliation was complete. And he was sure that coming back home had possibly been one of the biggest mistakes of his life.

Given the other poor choices he'd made in his life, that was saying quite a lot.

He sucked in a shaky breath, trying to calm himself somehow. Letting the air out slowly, he turned on his heel and headed down the deck stairs to the yard. Spying a wooden bench in the far corner, he trudged through the grass toward the bench, needing a moment alone.

He sat and unbuttoned his suit coat, then rubbed his hands over his face, feeling the burden of his past pressing down on him like a large weight. Every mistake he'd made had seemed to gather in one huge load since he'd come back home. Not surprising, really. He'd always known this transition wouldn't be easy. But he'd underestimated how awful it would feel to encounter such derision. At this moment, he really wondered if he were strong enough to stay in Moonlight Cove.

Just then, he saw his mom heading across the grass in his direction. She wore a very pretty navy blue-and-white flowered dress, a cream-colored, lacy sweater and sensible flats with bows on them. Her hair, which she'd cut short while he'd been in L.A., glinted with red tones in the autumn sunshine. Though she'd gained a bit of weight since he'd seen her last, she still looked good for a woman in her mid-fifties.

She drew to a stop a few yards from the bench. "Do you mind if I join you?"

He scooted over and patted the space next to him. "Not at all." He and his mother had reconnected somewhat over the telephone since he'd been through rehab, and he was glad. Dealing with his dad's contempt was bad enough. A strained relationship with his mom might push Curt over the edge.

She sat, then arranged the full skirt of her dress around herself. "You want to talk about what just happened?"

"You heard?"

"No, but Seth told me, and knowing Liz Woolsey, I can imagine plenty." She sniffed. "She's a real piece of work."

"I did treat Amanda horribly." Just the thought of being such a jerk filled him with hot-edged shame. "I was an idiot."

"Yes, you were. But lots of kids do things they shouldn't, and all that happened a long time ago." She pressed a hand to his arm. "You apologized. It was ungracious of Liz not to accept your apology."

His mom's words eased a bit of his pain. But more took its place when he recalled his father's reaction. Or, *non*reaction in this case. "Dad didn't stand up for me."

"I know," she said. "He's…a difficult man."

"You know that better than anyone."

"Yes, I'm afraid I do." She sighed, her breath shaking. "He's very hard to ignore." Her hands clenched in her lap and she seemed to be keeping her gaze averted.

He sensed she had something to say. "Mom, what's on your mind?"

She turned to Curt, her eyes shining with unshed tears. "I'll never forgive myself for letting him kick you out after your accident."

Curt blinked. "We've never talked about that."

"I know, but maybe we should."

"I've always had the impression you wanted to avoid the subject."

"I did. Because I was ashamed." She shook her head. "But now I need to tell you why I did what I did. It won't change anything, but I'll feel better."

"Okay." His drug counselor, Marv, would be proud of Curt's willingness to rehash a painful moment. Maybe he was getting stronger, after all.

"As you know, your dad and I had a very…tumultuous relationship."

"That's an understatement."

"Yes, I guess it is." She blinked several times. "Your father was larger than life, and very volatile."

"He liked to yell, and I remember a lot of slammed doors and stomping around." Curt recalled more than once hiding under the covers when his dad went on one of his rampages. Curt had been terrified. His father had never been physically abusive, but he had been loud and demanding and childish. "He was a bully."

"Exactly," his mother said. "After years and years of that, I learned that the best way to control his outbursts was to just give in to whatever he wanted. Not rock the boat, so to speak. Arguing set him off in the worst way."

"Is that what you did when he kicked me out?" Curt asked softly.

She bowed her head. "I wanted peace, and arguing wasn't going to get me that, and I thought that at eighteen you'd be fine."

"I was just a kid, Mom, and I was badly injured. How could you possibly think I'd be fine?"

Her face twisted. "I…I don't know. I guess I crumbled under pressure. That's lame, I know, but it's all I have." She swallowed. "I've always regretted what I did."

Curt thought about what she'd said. "I know how Dad can be."

"Can you forgive me?" she asked, her voice raspy. "I made a terrible mistake."

"I've made some of those," he replied, thinking aloud. "I'm the king of bad choices."

She stayed silent, but the agonized look on her face spoke volumes.

"Mom, one of the things my therapist taught me is that I need to be honest with people, and to quit holding things in and letting them fester." He leaned over and put his forearms on his knees, his gaze averted. "So, I need to say something."

"Okay."

"I've always resented you and Dad for ignoring us kids while we were growing up. I blamed you guys for everything, and used what happened as an excuse for my mistakes." He looked back at her.

She simply nodded, her lips trembling, her eyes glittering with unshed tears.

"Some of that was understandable, I guess. But I'm a grown man now, and I need to move on with my life and make something of myself. I need to quit using you and Dad as my excuse, or I'll never get where I want to be."

"So what are you saying?" she asked tentatively, as if she were scared to hear the rest.

He sat up, then reached out and took her hand in his. "What I'm saying is that I forgive you, Mom. I have to, or I'll forever be stuck in the same place."

With a muffled cry she put her arms around him and hugged him tight. "Oh, Curt. I can't tell you how happy this makes me."

He hugged her back, his own eyes burning. "I'm happy, too." At least one good thing had come out of today. "I want my family back."

"I want that, too," she said in a shaky voice.

Curt pulled away but kept hold of her hand. It felt good to be connected to her again. He'd been too long without a mom. One thought brought him down, though. "I'm not sure Dad is ever going to be a part of the family."

She wiped her damp cheeks. "He's a stubborn man, and he has his own mistakes to atone for. I hope he comes around and realizes how foolish he's being."

"Me, too." A thought occurred to Curt. "What made you come around on this?"

"Mainly the divorce."

"How so?"

"Well, I spent so much time trying to make your father happy, I lost focus on myself." His mother dug a tissue out of her sweater pocket and dabbed at her eyes. "Once I got the courage to leave and take care of my own needs, I realized that I'd been selfish and foolish, and that I wasn't going to be complete until I'd made amends and had my kids back in my life."

"So you're happy?"

"Yes, I am. It's not easy being single at my age, but I'm doing okay. I have a job I love, grand-babies and new friends to do things with."

"New male friends?" he asked with a quirk of his lips. "You have a lot of life left."

"No one special," she replied seriously. "It's not like there are a whole bunch of men my age here in Moonlight Cove." She turned a specula-tive gaze his way. "And how about you? Are you interested in anyone?"

"I'm not focusing on romance right now," he said. "Besides, I'm not sure any woman is going to be interested in a guy with my sketchy past."

"The key word being *past,* as in over and done with."

"Yes, that's one way to look at it." But Mrs. Woolsey had made it clear today that the past was not easily overlooked. "Hey, you're a kind, considerate, good-looking, eligible man with a lot to offer. I'm sure there will be lots of women interested in you."

But not Jenna. No way would he fit the qualifications on her perfect-man checklist. "Maybe someday I'll worry about that. Right now, I'm focused on recovery and rebuilding my life. That takes a lot of my energy."

"What about Jenna, the young woman who runs this place? She's very pretty, and she seems nice."

He tried not to look too shocked she'd brought up the very woman he'd just been thinking about. "She is nice. But she doesn't want a man like me."

"How do you know?"

"She has a list of things she wants in her next boyfriend, and somehow I don't think 'former drug addict' is on it."

"Does she know about your past problems with drugs?"

"Nope, and I'm not telling her anytime soon."

"Too ashamed?" his mother asked.

"You could say that."

"Well, I get that shame thing since I've had to deal with my fair share. But I've also found that

honesty is the best policy. If you're at all interested in her, you should tell her rather than risk
her finding out some other way."

He shifted on the hard bench as unease made
his gut clench. "I'll think about it."

The sound of a glass clinking from the deck
carried to Curt. "Sounds like they're getting ready
to cut the cake." He stood and held out his hand.
"You ready to go back up?"

His mom took his hand and rose. "Are you?"

He thought about that for a second. "Yes, I am."

"I think your dad's still here...."

"I'll deal with him as best I can. I'm not going
to let him run me off. I'll never recover fully if
I don't learn to deal with his negative attitude."

His mother squeezed his hand and fell in step
with him. "I admire your mind-set."

"Well, it's been a long time coming," he said.

"Yes, it has. I'm proud of you, Curt. You've
overcome a lot, and are really focused on getting
the things you want."

Something in the vicinity of his heart melted.
"Thanks, Mom. I never thought I'd hear you say
that."

"If you ever need anything, I'm here."

"I know, Mom."

The wind picked up and ruffled his hair. As
he and his mother approached the festivities, he

looked skyward at the puffy white clouds scudding across the blue sky. A prayer rose in his mind.

Thank You, Lord, for bringing my mom back into my life. Now, if You could just help me find the wisdom and strength to weather the storm with Dad I'd be grateful. I fear he'll never be proud of me, or be a part of my life. And the man I've become would mourn the loss deeply.

Chapter Six

With her back screaming, Jenna folded up another chair and put it in the stack she'd made by
the door. She'd been on her feet fourteen hours
and counting. She was completely exhausted.
But the weatherman was calling for rain over-
night, and she had to get the tables, chairs and
tablecloths she'd rented into the garage or risk
them getting soaked. There was still work to be
done, and she'd been raised to carry on no matter what.

Thankfully, the reception had gone wonder-
fully—Phoebe had been thrilled with every aspect
of Jenna's work. If she built a steady catering and
guest clientele, the inn would get the maintenance
it needed to stay in business.

Just as she had the next chair folded up, the
screen door opened. Curt. With Miss Landry already in her room, asleep, who else would it be?

"What are you doing out here in the dark?" he asked.

She swung her gaze toward him. "Cleaning up."

He'd changed from the suit he'd worn for the wedding festivities into a pair of worn jeans and a short-sleeved T-shirt. Though he'd looked good—really, really good—in the charcoal-gray suit, snow-white dress shirt and light blue tie, she much preferred this more casual attire on him.

Maybe that was because these clothes showed off his arms rather than covering them up....

She scowled slightly. Obviously, her exhaustion had gotten the better of her.

"Can't it wait until tomorrow?" he asked, coming closer.

"Nope. It's going to rain, and I don't want this stuff to get wet." She folded the chair, wincing. "Besides, I have church in the morning and grocery shopping later in the day, along with my usual weekend chores, and I need to go see Grams. I won't have time."

He came closer, his brow creased in concern. "Is your back still hurting you?"

"A bit," she said, downplaying. Actually, it felt as if the muscles in her upper back were on fire. "I'll live."

"I'm sure you will." He paused, his head cocked. "I'm guessing you don't want me to help."

She yanked a tablecloth off. "You would be right."

He stood there for a moment, then without a word went over and started stacking chairs.

"Hey." She frowned. "I don't want you doing that."

"I'm aware of your feelings on the subject," he replied in an even voice.

She blinked. "So…you're just going to ignore me?"

"I'm just doing work that needs to be done." He hefted three chairs into the pile, causing the muscles in his back and shoulders to ripple.

Her mouth went dry. "You really—" She cleared her throat. "Um, you really don't have to help."

"I know." He went over and grabbed some more chairs. "But I want to. You've been on your feet all day and look like you're ready to drop."

"I can do it," she said, lifting her chin, her fingers gripping the tablecloth in her hands.

"I know you can, and you will." Up went the chairs. His shoulders worked again in that fascinating way, bunching under his shirt. "But I'm here, and I prefer to keep busy."

She kept her gaze focused on his face. "Idle hands?"

"You have no idea," he replied with a lift of his brow.

That sounded interesting. "Care to elaborate?" Making conversation was good.

"Let's just say I don't like to have a lot of downtime," he said, his voice tinged with curtness.

Technically, he'd given a nonanswer, yet his tight tone implied a wealth of feeling lay behind his statement. Her curiosity surged, adding to her interest in the incident she'd witnessed earlier with Mrs. Woolsey.

Jenna had been in the house when the conversation had started, so she hadn't caught everything the woman had said. But Jenna had heard enough to understand the gist of the woman's "discussion" with Curt. The words *deplorable behavior* and something about polluted air had been hard to miss, and had, honestly, sent shock waves through Jenna.

It was becoming clear Curt had a checkered history in Moonlight Cove, and her nosy side would love to know the details. But…grilling him would be rude, no matter how much the implications in his tone raised her inquisitiveness. And she was determined not to be nosy.

Clamping her interest and her mouth tight, she grabbed another tablecloth, then looked at him again. "You're a stubborn man." Enigmatic, too. Intriguing combination. Not that she was intrigued, per se….

"Only when I come up against someone even more stubborn."

"I am not stubborn," she said with a lift of her chin. "Just…independent." She'd learned to get along at the inn without much help out of necessity. Get 'er done was the Flaherty family motto.

"That, too," he said. "And, by the way, you did a great job here today."

His praise let loose a fluttery feeling. "Thanks." She beamed and caught his gaze. Instantly something passed between them, something that held her in place, and had her tummy flipping circles.

Finally he cleared his throat and looked away. "Um…all of your hard work paid off, didn't it?" he said, his voice sounding hoarse.

"I think it did." She smoothed the pile of folded tablecloths, hoping he didn't see how her hands shook. "Working so hard isn't easy, but it's rewarding." Nothing would make her happier than making sure the Sweetheart remained solvent. Failing Grams wasn't happening.

"Yeah, I really admire your work ethic."

She looked at him, trying not to get too caught up in his commending her. "You do?"

"Yep. It gives me inspiration."

Okay, that was a loaded answer, one that raised his intrigue factor sky-high. "Why do you need inspiration?" She kept her tone conversational, taking care not to sound as if she was snooping.

He started another stack of chairs. "I had some…ups and downs in L.A., and I'm refocusing my life to more…balanced endeavors."

Interesting. More balanced endeavors? And what did *ups and downs* mean? Asking the question would seem like prying, so instead she posed, "What's L.A. like? I've never been there." Her parents had maintained packed work schedules and had rarely taken time off, so they weren't travelers. Jenna had never left the Pacific Northwest.

"Aside from nice weather, you're not missing much." He paused, then turned and regarded her, a shadow growing in his eyes. "It has plenty of distractions but no heart to speak of."

"Ah, I see. Big and impersonal?"

"Very. That works for some lifestyles, and I loved it when I was younger." He picked up the final two chairs and added them to the stack. "But, ultimately, I decided that I needed a more stable environment."

"It sounds like L.A. is the polar opposite of Moonlight Cove."

"Exactly."

"That's one of the things I love about this town." She gathered up the pile of tablecloths. "I've always felt so at home here."

"Interesting, because I never did."

She pulled in her chin. "Really?"

"Really," he replied, his jaw noticeably tight.

Interesting. "Does that have anything to do with Mrs. Woolsey's reaction to you?"

He froze and stared at her for a long, silent moment. "You heard the whole thing?"

She nodded. "Pretty much."

Leaning over, he placed his hands on the table and hung his head for a moment.

The motion had regret bouncing through her. "I'm sorry," she said hastily. "I shouldn't have brought that up."

"No, it's a valid question." He straightened. "As you probably gathered, I dated Mrs. Woolsey's daughter in high school, and the relationship ended badly."

"You don't have to tell me this." But, oh, was she ever curious. Who wouldn't be?

"Yes, I do," he said, his voice coated in steel. "The truth is, I treated Amanda terribly back then. I was a total jerk."

"I'm having a hard time imagining you like that." He'd only ever been kind and decent to her, Miss Landry and Sam.

"Oh, trust me, it's true." He scrubbed a hand over his face. "I was full of myself, and had a chip on my shoulder as big as a house."

"Why such a big chip?"

"Partly because I was a teenage boy who questioned everything. And partly—mostly, I guess—because my dad and I have never seen eye to eye, to put it mildly." His lips thinned. "I figured if I couldn't please him, no matter what I did, why even try."

Something began to make sense. "He was here today, wasn't he?" She'd seen the tall, sun-burned, gray-haired man arrive, and had thought he looked familiar. Because he looked like Curt, and Seth, too. There was a definite family resemblance there.

"Yep, he was," Curt said in a quiet voice that held an edge of strain.

More pieces fell into place, and her chest tightened. "I saw him out on the patio," she said, moving closer. "He didn't defend you, did he?"

"He did not." Three short words, yet they were long on explanation and rife with pain.

She sucked in a breath, feeling his hurt. "So, you haven't worked things out with him."

"No, and after today, I'm not sure we ever will."

Her heart turned over. "Maybe it will just take some time."

"Maybe," Curt replied with a tilt of his head. "Maybe not."

"But he's your dad...." Her parents, with all of their quirks and need for perfection, had always shown her unconditional love.

"That should matter, right?"

His statement packed a punch, and a sick feeling spread through her. She worked her jaw.

He shook his head. "But I've done a lot of things to disappoint him, and I'm not sure we'll ever find a way to bridge the gap."

She resisted the urge to reach out and touch Curt, comfort him. Talking was one thing. Making physical contact another. She wouldn't dream of crossing that line—she barely knew him. "Surely you haven't given up hope?"

He picked up a load of chairs as if they were as light as a feather. "No, I'll always have hope. But hopes don't always come true, and some rifts are too wide to ever close."

She didn't know what to say to that, so she simply nodded.

"Well, I'm done with the chairs, so I think I'll head in and hit the hay."

"Okay, good night," she said.

"Good night." With those words echoing in the still, chilly night air, he turned and headed into the house.

Her tummy twisting at his statement, Jenna stood alone with her churning thoughts. Between Mrs. Woolsey's beyond rude yet illuminating outburst, Curt's hints at wanting a more balanced life and his confession about his relationship with his dad, it was becoming apparent Curt was a wounded man with an…um…*interesting* past. But rather than cooling her interest in him…that revelation simply fueled it even higher.

Chapter Seven

Curt stared up at the ceiling in his room, illuminated by the light of the moon shining in through the window. The large oak tree outside cast weird, shifting shadows on the walls, and he could smell the ocean breeze through the window he'd left open a crack before he'd turned in.

He muttered something under his breath, threw an arm over his head and tried to get comfortable, forcing himself not to look at the digital clock on the nightstand; it was only ten minutes or so later than the last time he'd checked.

He frowned. Struggling to sleep usually wasn't an issue for him. But tonight? Well, tonight, all he could think about was the conversation he'd had with Jenna just a few hours ago.

Try as he might, he couldn't forget the way her jaw had dropped when he'd revealed the true nature of his relationship with his dad. Shame had marched through him like an army of fire ants, and though the emotion was sickeningly familiar, he still hated it, hated how powerless it made him feel, how vulnerable and sad.

He had no idea why he'd shared so much with her. He usually kept stuff—particularly anything to do with his family—pretty close to the vest. He'd been raised by experts to put up and shut up, and breaking that pattern was hard. He'd never even told his last girlfriend where his parents lived, much less about his rocky relationship with his dad.

So what was it about Jenna that had made him want to talk? Sure, she asked the right questions, and she was a good listener. But what else called to him in such a way that he was willing to share his past with her? Or at least parts of it?

Suddenly warm, he shifted, then flung the covers off and sat up, throwing his feet over the side of the bed. Swiping a hand through his hair, he hung his head, his emotions jostling for space in his mind. The room closed in, smothering him like a heavy blanket.

He jerked to his feet and headed to the window. Pushing it open, he took a big swig of fresh air, trying to clear his head. The tang of the ocean sluiced through his head, clearing things a bit. But he still felt restless and edgy.

Obviously, sleep wasn't happening. Not with so

much on his mind. Out of the corner of his eye he saw a shadow on the floor to his left. His guitar. Maybe playing would calm him down. Usually, his music soothed him, helped him gain perspective. He needed that now. He saw the porch down below him, illuminated by the light still burning by the front door. If he remembered right, there was seating on that porch. He could play down there, free from his too-warm bed and the small bedroom's shrinking walls. He needed space, room to clear his head.

His mind made up, he turned, pulled on a pair of sweatpants and a long-sleeved T-shirt. He grabbed his guitar and headed downstairs, keeping his tread light on the wooden risers leading to the foyer so as not to wake Jenna or Miss Landry.

The house was quiet and dark, save for a pair of lamps glowing from each end of a table in the hallway, and the porch light, which cast weak yellow light into the foyer through the narrow, etched-glass windows flanking the door.

Silently he made his way to the door and unlocked the dead bolt and handle lock. Hoping Jenna kept the hinges well oiled, he eased it open, squinting. Blessedly, it was squeak free. Sighing in relief, he slipped outside and closed it inaudibly behind him.

Once he was out on the porch, his tension eased a bit more. A light mist had coated the grass, and the air was cool yet refreshing. Frogs croaked from somewhere in the yard, their throaty chorus breaking the stillness of the night with their serenade.

He sat in the gliding rocker in the corner, and then turned his attention to his guitar. With no particular song in mind, he simply strummed chords, one after the other, humming along.

Once he'd worked the kinks out of his fingers, he seamlessly segued into the chords for one of his favorite songs, "Michael Row the Boat Ashore," a song he'd heard for the first time just a few months ago at a church retreat. He strummed the chords for a while, closing his eyes, letting the music work its way into his brain like a soothing lullaby.

He smiled and softly began to sing about Michael and his sister rowing the boat ashore across the deep, wide river Jordan toward their home on the other side.

Along about the third chorus, he looked up from the guitar and saw Jenna step out onto the porch dressed in a fluffy pink robe belted at the waist and fuzzy slippers on her feet.

He froze, his heart jumping, and his fingers slipped from the proper fret, his guitar emitting a discordant mishmash of notes. He cringed and quit playing.

"Why are you stopping?" she asked, her voice soft and low.

"Um…you startled me," he said lamely, his cheeks warming. He hadn't expected to see her, though part of him was glad she'd sought him out.

She cocked a brow. "You must have been lost in the song."

"Yeah, I guess I was." He shrugged. "I've never been good at singing in front of others."

She moved closer, and the muted illumination cast from the porch light gilded her unbound hair with copper highlights. "Did you play in a band when you lived in L.A.?"

"Yes, the key word being *play*. I played but didn't sing." He wouldn't tell her he'd always been too high during gigs to keep track of lyrics.

"You should have," she said. "You have a very good voice."

Her praise lit up a warm space in his heart that he realized in hindsight had been cold a long time. Interesting how a guy didn't know what had been missing until it was right in front of him. "Thanks."

She sank into one of the chairs flanking the glider, pulling her robe tight around her legs. "Please continue," she said with a slight tilt of her head. "I love this song."

"It's one of my favorites, too," he replied, liking that they had their love of the song in common.

"So, play it for me. We can enjoy it together."

He'd been by himself for so long, just the sound of the word *together* made his gut clench. He didn't share much with others, though he was trying to change that. But…could he really play—and sing—for her? "Er…I usually play by myself," he said, falling back on what was easy. Safe.

"Can you make an exception?" She settled back, her eyes resting lightly on him. "I really like what I've heard so far."

He cocked his head at her in question. "How long were you listening?"

"My room is right above the porch, and I always sleep with my window open, so I heard you from the beginning."

The thought of her listening had a weird feeling flaring inside, a combination of pleasure and anxiety, mixed together to throw him just off-balance.

He paused, more nerves sparking.

She began to rise. "If you don't want to, I understand…."

"No, no." He motioned her to sit. "I'll play." In the interest of personal growth—and maybe something else he didn't want to put his finger on—he'd share this with her. "Are you sure I won't wake Miss Landry?"

"I doubt it," Jenna replied. "She told me she sleeps very soundly."

"All right, then." He put his fingers in the position for the C major chord, and suddenly, his hands felt clumsy, as if they were fat sausages instead of appendages under his control. He closed his eyes for a second, and sucked in a breath and then let it out. Instantly, his tight, clumsy fingers eased up.

He started strumming in the down, down, up rhythm he preferred for the song, and tentatively, began to sing, hoping his voice wouldn't crack. He kept his eyes down, on his left hand, as he concentrated on making the chords. He felt if he looked at Jenna, met her emerald gaze, he'd flub, and for some reason, he wanted the song to be perfect for her.

He sang three verses, each one getting easier as he got into the rhythm and relaxed. Still focusing on his left hand, he ended on the chorus, strumming with a flourish. The final chord echoed in the quiet night, drowning out even the sound of the frogs.

For just a moment, silence reigned, and he was afraid that she hadn't liked the song, though why that mattered was a mystery. He was afraid to look up, afraid to see her reaction.

"That was beautiful," she said in a hushed voice.

Relief spread through him; clearly, her approval was important, though, right now, he'd ignore the implications of that realization. He looked up and met her soft gaze. "Thanks. Though as songs go, it's an easy one."

"Sometimes the easy, less flashy songs are the best."

"Yeah, I guess you're right." He turned her comment over in his mind. "Though the song isn't complicated, the melody and words always lift me up."

"Me, too." She nodded slowly. "So I take it the song…resonates with you," she said, cutting right to the chase.

"Yes, it does."

"Care to explain?" she asked, leaning forward, her hands folded in her lap, her gaze direct. Ah, *there* was the chase…

Her interest had his old walls creeping up, and he almost threw out something flip to avoid talking. Deflecting, his counselor had called the technique. Dutifully, Curt recalled what Marv had said:

Curt, you'll never get where you want to be unless you learn to communicate.

He had his path laid out, had all of the tools at his disposal, tools he would never learn how to use unless he practiced. So he swallowed and said, "I've been in my own boat, rowing home against a deep, wide river."

After a pause, she nodded. "Is the shore in sight?" she questioned in a steady voice.

"I think so, yes." He strummed a random chord.

"Sometimes the shore is hard to see."

He placed his hand on the guitar strings to quiet them. "You sound like you have experience with distant shores."

"Yes, with me running the inn, expectations are high." She smiled, but it didn't reach her eyes. "My own personal deep river, so to speak."

"Your own expectations?"

"Yes, mine, and my family's, too."

He narrowed his eyes. "So your family expects a lot of you."

"Oh, yeah." She shifted on her chair. "Everyone in my family is perfect."

"No one is perfect."

"My parents and my brother are," she said with quiet authority.

"You're kidding, right?"

"Not at all. They set their sights on something, and they do it. Really well." Her mouth turned downward slightly. "Without fail."

"Wow." He rubbed his jaw. "That's a lot to live up to."

"I know."

The true picture was beginning to emerge. "So that's why you work so hard around here?"

"I have to," she replied. "Flahertys don't fail."

"I know what it's like constantly trying to

please other people." And what it was like to never succeed.

"Yes, it is. But I'm used to living up to high standards," she said, a hint of stoicism in her voice.

Ah, yes, those high standards again. "Do you ever believe you're doing your best, and that's enough?"

She paused. "Sometimes."

"You should believe it all the time," he said with conviction as he remembered Marv's whole believing-in-oneself credo.

"I try."

"Good." He hesitated. "I'm guessing that's why you have a perfect-man checklist."

Her brow creased. "Perfect-man checklist?"

"Yeah, you know, the list Miss Landry and you were talking about the other day." It seemed she had high standards for every part of her life.

"Oh, yeah, that. I came up with that list after I let myself fall for the wrong guy and had my heart broken." She raised her chin. "I want to avoid another romantic failure at all costs."

"Someone broke your heart?"

"Yes, my college boyfriend." Her jaw visibly tightened. "He, um, cheated on me."

"Oh, wow, I'm sorry." He'd done some pretty crummy things, but he'd never cheated. "Past mistakes have a way of teaching us lessons, don't they?" He was an expert on that particular idea. He was just a slow learner.

"Yes, they do. After Garrett cheated on me, I learned that I need to be careful, thoughtful and picky about love."

Careful. Thoughtful. Picky. Made sense. And ruled Curt out. His gut tightened. "So you want perfection in love, too," he stated.

"Yes. Just as all the Flahertys have." She smiled brightly. "I just have to have faith I'll eventually find my perfect love."

"Ah, yes, I'm familiar with that faith concept." Marv had drilled in the faith-in-oneself thing like a sledgehammer, and Curt had done his best to withstand the blows. And learn from them. But a lifetime of little faith was hard to ignore.

She peered at him, her brows knit. "So it's just a concept to you?"

Curt chewed on the inside of his cheek. Sharing the truth with her would be difficult. But he reminded himself again, that part of his therapy was to learn to open up instead of letting things fester and eat away at him. "In my childhood, faith of any kind was in short supply." He laughed abruptly, which came out more of a snort. "Non-existent, actually."

"Oh, no," she said, leaning her arms on her knees. "Does it have something to do with your dad?"

Curt's back teeth ground together. "It has *everything* to do with my dad."

She stayed quiet, clearly waiting for him to go on.

"My parents had a very…turbulent relationship." He set his guitar down on the glider seat. "They were always so caught up in fighting that they neglected my brothers and me." He did his best to keep his voice even. Calm, when he felt anything but.

"That must have been so hard for you guys."

The sympathy in her tone made his throat tighten, and for just a moment he had an overwhelming urge to follow old habits and simply get up and walk away. He hated getting emotional.

But…he had to stay and talk if he had any hope of learning how to deal with life's challenges. He had to face down the things that scared him or he'd never have the life he wanted, free of the negative things that had helped him cope in the past.

He had to learn to rely on himself.

"It was," he finally said, making himself step through the door she'd opened. "We were on our own a lot, and we learned early on to just deal with whatever came our way."

Her mouth turned downward. "I'm so sorry your parents weren't there for you."

"Everyone has problems, I know that. And we never starved or didn't have a roof over our heads."

"But emotionally...?" she asked, a rasp in her tone.

"Emotionally, we didn't have much support." He managed to say it without his voice cracking, which was a victory.

After a pause, she asked, "And your lack of faith growing up? How does that fit in?"

That answer was easy though heartbreaking. "If someone has no faith in their parents, any other kind of faith is pretty much impossible to find."

She blinked, stared, but said nothing.

"I can see you're shocked," he said through thinned lips. Maybe he shouldn't have opened up.

"Not shocked. More like...incredibly sad."

He stiffened. "I don't want your pity."

"Being sad for what someone went through isn't pity."

He thought about that, his eyes on the floor of the porch, his neck muscles bunched. His defenses were always quick to rise. He needed to work on that. Regret burned through him.

Her slippered feet appeared in his line of vision. "You see the difference, don't you?" she asked, her voice whisper-soft.

"Yes, I do, and I'm sorry for getting defensive."

He rubbed his neck and moved his head side to side, stretching the tight muscles. "It's one of my biggest faults."

"Well, if that's the case, I'm not sure we can be friends anymore."

His gaze flew up to her face and a lump of disappointment settled in his gut. "Really?"

She gave him a chiding look. "No, not really, silly. I'm being facetious."

Relief spread in a warming tide through him. "Oh, okay." He'd never been good at reading social cues, though he was working on the skill. He was a black-and-white kind of guy. In between had always been hard for him.

"My point being, we all have faults—yes, even me—and that's nothing to be ashamed about."

"What are your faults?" he asked, doubting there were any. She seemed pretty perfect to him.

"Well, I'm stubborn, and I don't like to accept help. And I don't get enough sleep. But I'm working on that." Bringing that point home, she stifled a yawn. "Oh, goodness me. I guess my day is finally catching up with me."

"Yes, you need to work on that sleep thing."

"What about you?" she asked, concern creasing her brow. "You had a long day, too. You ought to get some rest."

He couldn't remember the last time someone other than his therapist had been genuinely worried about him. Something akin to exhilaration thrummed through him, but he tried not to let himself get too tangled up in why. "I'm going to stay out here a bit more." He was still too keyed up to sleep. "Don't worry, I won't disturb you."

"I'm not worried about that at all." She headed for the door and stopped, turning, swinging her hair behind her. "Maybe a song will lull me to sleep."

He picked up his guitar, trying to veer away from thinking about her listening to him from her room. "Then in that case, I'll think of a lullaby to play."

"Perfect." She paused, her gaze meeting his and holding for a second.

His heart hammered against his ribs and his breathing went shallow.

After a second or two she spoke. "Oh, um, I was going to ask you, would you like to go to church with me tomorrow?"

He cleared his throat. "I'd love to," he said honestly. "Going to a new church is intimidating, so it'll be nice to attend with a friend."

"New church? So you didn't go to church here in Moonlight Cove when you were growing up?"

"Nope. My parents didn't take us." Any kind of family activity was rare, and neither of his parents were believers.

"But you've found God?"

"Yes, just recently." As part of rehab. Not that he'd tell her that; he didn't just bandy about his addiction history. Not even the recovery part.

Jenna's lips curved up into a gentle smile. "Great. The service starts at nine, so why don't we leave right after breakfast."

"Sounds good." Something eased inside of him, and he realized that he'd been worried about going to church in a new place. Bless Jenna for her invitation. Although, now that he thought about it, Seth and Kim would probably be there. But it was too late to call and confirm that.

Jenna opened the door. "Breakfast is at seven-thirty on Sundays."

"You don't have to cook for me," he said, putting his feet flat on the porch floor.

"Yes, I do."

His breathing hitched. "Why?"

"Because it's included in your room rate," she said, scrunching up her nose.

"Ah, of course." He was being foolish to think she meant something else.

"Okay, then, I'll see you in the morning." With a wave and a shy smile, she left the porch, leaving him with memories of the moment her gaze had locked with his own and he'd almost quit breathing.

He liked Jenna Flaherty. A lot.

Too bad. He knew he would never meet her

high standards. A woman like her would never be interested in a guy with his past.

In the silence, the frogs' croaking floated to him on the breeze. And fittingly, their song no longer sounded like a joyful chorus; it simply sounded sad and lonely.

Chapter Eight

With dead-of-night silence echoing around her, Jenna lay in bed, waiting to hear the lullaby Curt had promised. Inevitably, her thoughts went back to their conversation out on the porch.

Her heart clenched. His story about his mom and dad had made her so sad. And his statement about how hard it was growing up with no faith in anything when you had no faith in your parents had hollowed her out.

He'd had a rough childhood, one that had to have left scars. And his mom and dad's problems had, by his own admission, led to sketchy faith.

His own deep, wide river was becoming clear. A lifetime of family dysfunction. Faith issues. A dad who was still neglecting his son.

What a complicated man Curt was. She punched her pillow and turned over, letting her mind drift to her "perfect-man list," as Curt had called it. She had never made an actual written list. Nothing as formal as that. But she definitely had a mental list going. It included an uncomplicated man with a healthy mental outlook. Deep familial ties. Abiding faith, both in himself and in God. A clear levelheadedness and stability.

Her mind swung back to Curt. He was clearly damaged. Who wouldn't be after his upbringing? In truth, he met none of her criteria. He didn't fit the bill.

But something about him called to her—

The soft, sweet strains of an expertly played guitar drifted to her through her open window. The tune was familiar: "Brahms Lullaby," which her mother used to sing to her.

Holding her breath, Jenna strained to hear the words that Curt sang:

Good evening, good night. With roses adorned, With carnations covered, slip under the covers.
Early tomorrow, if God wills, you will wake once again.
Early tomorrow, if God wills, you will wake once again.

His smooth, silky voice flowed over her as he sang the second verse. Entranced, she laid stock-still, the pillow clutched between her fingers, taking small breaths so she wouldn't miss one second of the song.

Soon—too soon—the song ended. But Curt

kept playing the guitar, and the sweet strains of the chords washed over her.

All thoughts of her list fled. Only to be replaced by two profound questions:

Given Curt's complicated past, was it possible he might be the man she was looking for?

And how would she ever be sure?

Jenna put the last of the dishes in the dishwasher after Sunday dinner with Curt and Miss Landry.

Curt finished wiping the counters, then brought the sponge over to the sink to rinse it out. "Great dinner," he said. "I love pot roast."

Jenna smiled, trying not to notice how his hair fell down over his brow. Or how much she wanted to sweep it back with her fingers. "Thanks. Grams taught me to make it."

"She was a good cook, I take it?"

"The best cook I've ever known. Some of my best memories are from cooking with her in this kitchen." Maybe that was why Jenna spent so much time in the kitchen now; doing so reminded her of Grams.

He leaned a hip against the counter. "You love this house, don't you?"

"I do." She squirted the soap into the dishwasher and closed it. "I always felt more at home here than at my real home."

Curt tilted his head a bit. "Did you have a bad life growing up?"

"Oh, no, not at all." She closed the dishwasher and turned it on. "But my family is very…high-energy, very focused on doing as much as possible every day, with little downtime. High achievers every one of them." Jenna scraped a stray crumb into the sink. "I always felt more relaxed here. Grams and Gramps worked hard, but they really took time to savor life. There were lazy afternoons on the beach. Nights spent working on jigsaw puzzles. Stuff like that." They'd always taken time to talk to her, too, and not just in passing, as her parents were more wont to do.

"No wonder you liked it here so much," Curt replied. "Your grandparents sound like wonderful people."

"Definitely."

"How did your visit with her today go?"

"It was okay." Jenna had gone to Oakhurst Memory Care to see Grams after church today, as she did every Sunday.

"Just okay?"

"Well, Grams was in good spirits, as she usually is." A streak of sadness shot through Jenna. "But the Alzheimer's makes it so she barely recognizes me anymore."

"So while the visit was as good as it could be, it was still hard."

She hung the dish towel on its bar next to the sink. "Right. She really isn't the same Grams I once knew." A lump of grief, heavy and hard, formed in her chest. She missed the old Grams badly.

"I'm sorry," he said.

"Thanks."

He paused for a moment. "I wanted to tell you that I really enjoyed church today. Thank you for going with me."

"My pleasure." It had been really nice sitting next to Curt, worshipping. "I thought the sermon was really well done." Pastor Goodrich had preached about keeping faith through trials and tribulations.

"Me, too. And very timely, too."

"Has your newfound faith wavered lately?" she asked, taking off her apron.

"No, but it's nice to know what to do if it ever does."

Just then, the phone rang. Jenna checked the clock on the wall. Exactly 6:30 p.m. "That's my mom calling to check on Grams. I could set my clock by her." She hung her apron up and headed to the phone. "Excuse me."

Curt nodded and pointed upstairs, indicating he was going to his room.

Jenna returned his nod and picked the cordless phone up, pressing Talk. "Hi, Mom."

"Hi, sweetie. Are you done with dinner?"

"Yep, just finished cleaning up."

"Oh, good."

They talked about Grams for a few minutes, and discussed the billing error Oakhurst had made and how Jenna and her mom were going to resolve it. Mom, who had power of attorney, paid the bills for Grams's care from Grams's account, so Mom was going to call Oakhurst to get more information.

"So, how's Dad?" Jenna asked.

"He's good. Working long hours at the university as usual. But he found time to finish the new patio last weekend, before the rain sets in. He started with a new trainer at the gym last week, too." Her dad ran marathons and was constantly tweaking his training routine.

Her mom went on, "And we agreed to host the annual staff Christmas party again this year, so that will keep us busy during the holidays."

Jenna nodded. "Business as usual with you guys."

"Yes, I guess so. You know we like to keep busy. Oh, and we've been golfing a lot, so your dad's happy."

Her father was a scratch golfer, and her mother had a really low handicap, as well. They skied in the winter, and played tennis—excellently, of course—at the club they belonged to. Her brother,

Scott, had been the state champion in tennis three years running in high school, as well as an all-American soccer player. He'd had to decide between a stint on a semipro soccer team or law school. He'd chosen law school—Harvard, of course—and was on track to be the youngest person to ever make partner in the law firm for which he worked.

Jenna, on the other hand, had two left feet and had been a theater geek in high school.

Pretty paltry in comparison to her superparents and bionic brother.

She brought her attention back to the conversation at hand. "Didn't you guys play in a couples tournament last week?" Her mom had mentioned it last Sunday.

"Yes, we did, and we won our age bracket!"

Not surprising. Her parents won just about every tournament they entered. "That's great."

"Scott and Julie played with us, and they won their bracket, too." Julie was Scott's wife. They were also excellent golfers, and both routinely crushed the competition. They were a gorgeous couple, who'd fallen in love in college, married seven years ago and now had a couple of gorgeous children. All with nary a hitch to be seen.

"How do they have time to golf, what with the new baby?" Jenna's niece, London, had been born just a few months ago, joining Jenna's barely two-year-old nephew, Peyton. Having two kids under the age of two hadn't seemed to stop Scott and Julie from tearing it up on the golf course. Jenna often wondered how they juggled two full-time law careers, maintained a beautiful home and managed two kids, all the while staying fit, happy and sane.

She felt like a lazy underachiever in comparison.

"Julie's sister Danielle took the kids for a few hours so Scott and Julie could play."

A wave of downheartedness washed over Jenna. "Sounds like they're living the dream." With ease and aplomb and little effort, it seemed.

How had she ended up the only Flaherty not to be blessed with the ability to blithely succeed at everything she set her mind to?

"Yes, I guess they are," her mom said. "They're leaving for Hawaii day after tomorrow."

"Oh, good for them," Jenna forced out.

"So. Any romantic prospects on the horizon for you?" Mom always asked this question. And Jenna always gave the same answer—no.

But something made her say, "Actually, an interesting guy is staying at the inn right now."

"Oh, really?" An edge of excitement sounded in Mom's voice. "What's he like?"

"He's very nice, and very handsome."

"Why is he staying at the inn?"

"He grew up here, and has been living in L.A. His brother owns the Sports Shack on Main Street, and Curt is here to run the place while his brother is in Seattle opening up a new store."

"Ah, I see." A pause. "Sounds like you like him."

"I do," Jenna said truthfully. She sat in one of the chairs by the table.

"Are you interested in dating him?"

"Um…I'm not sure."

"Why not? He sounds perfect."

"Well, he has a bit of a complicated past," Jenna said carefully. She wasn't comfortable sharing the exact details of Curt's misspent youth; her mom might not approve, and to Jenna, passing on what she'd witnessed at the wedding reception smacked of gossip. She wasn't going there.

"How so?" her mom asked, her voice rife with curiosity.

"Well…" How to put it? "Um…he got into a bit of trouble when he was younger."

"Oh, well, lots of people make mistakes in their youth."

"You didn't. Dad didn't. Scott didn't."

"You didn't, either," Mom said.

"I made a huge mistake not being more cautious with Garrett. I learned my lesson about jumping into a relationship headfirst without much thought. I let my heart rule my head and paid the price. I don't want to do that again."

"Garrett had his issues, certainly, so you're being cautious this time, to protect yourself."

"Right," Jenna said, nodding succinctly. "I'm being picky."

"Well, I guess that makes sense, given what's happened in the past."

"Exactly." Her mom was rarely wrong, so her agreement reinforced Jenna's strategy. She was doing the right thing by keeping her interest off Curt. She was sure of it.

Jenna exchanged end-of-conversation pleasantries with her mom and then hung up. She sat for a moment, recounting in her mind bits and pieces of her conversation.

Talk of the golf wins, the wonderful vacations, jobs and hobbies came back to her. The family tradition of perfect relationships that were precisely in sync with flawless, well-rounded lives held strong. With everyone but her.

She was the only Flaherty who'd struggled. She'd failed with Garrett and was barely treading water with the inn. She'd be lucky to be able to afford any kind of vacation ever.

As was usual after her phone calls with her mom, Jenna felt letdown and slightly blue.

No matter how hard she tried, she would never be like the rest of her family. But she had to try.

And that was one more reason so keep her heart well guarded from Curt.

Flahertys never failed. She had to remember that.

Chapter Nine

❧

Almost a week after Curt arrived in town, just when he'd thought he had the hang of running the store, he had a particularly challenging day at work. Oscar Morton had tried to return a fly-fishing rod without a receipt, and had been mad about Curt enforcing the official store policy, which clearly stated that all returns without receipt were eligible for store credit only.

Then the UPS delivery had arrived only partially filled and two customers' special orders hadn't arrived on time. Curt had spent an hour on the phone tracking the orders down, and both had been delayed due to bad weather in the Midwest. More unhappy customers.

Finally, the ancient toilet in the store's customer restroom had overflowed. Seth had left the number for the plumber, and luckily the guy had been able to come in and fix the problem quickly.

Despite the issues that had cropped up, Curt felt strangely content as he returned to the inn. He was facing and dealing with complications at the store, and he was proud of what he'd accomplished today. Now, if he could just get the hang of the Daily Sales Balance Sheet he had to fill out every day, he'd be golden.

Provided the plumbing didn't explode again anytime soon.

He stepped into the foyer, only to be bowled over by one happy seven-year-old boy.

"Mr. Graham!" Sam squealed, ramming his head into Curt's solar plexus.

"Oof." Curt doubled over, then caught his breath. "Whoa, bud, watch the old breadbasket."

Sam backed up and looked up at Curt, clearly perplexed. His eyes then darted to Curt's torso. "You have a breadbasket in you?"

Curt chuckled. "No, it's an expression that means stomach." He thought back to the game Operation that he and his brothers used to play, and the funny breadbasket plopped right in the middle of the patient's stomach.

To this day, Curt was proud that he was the only one of the three to successfully take the piece of bread—known far and wide as the most challenging "surgical" removal in the game—without setting off the buzzer. He'd earned a thousand points for that baby, and had won the game by a landslide, along with bragging rights for all time.

"Oh," Sam said, his nose crinkled. "Why is it called that?"

"Not sure, just is." The smell of roasting meat wafted to him. "Mmm. Something smells good."

Sam ran down the hardwood floor leading from the foyer to the kitchen and slid a good six feet on his socks. "Miss Jenna's making chicken. And taters. And green beans."

"Sounds great," Curt said, his stomach growling. He'd been so busy at the Sports Shack he hadn't eaten lunch, so he was starving.

Sam skated back toward Curt. "No dessert tonight, though."

"That's too bad, but dessert is only fun if you don't get it all the time." Curt followed his nose to the kitchen.

"Not to me," Sam replied, following Curt, jumping sideways. "Guess what?"

"What?" Curt passed the dining room, noting the table was already set for dinner.

"I was good all day today, so I get to work on my times tables with you tonight."

"That's great, Sam!" Last night at dinner, Curt had promised to help Sam with his multiplication tables if he cooperated with Jenna today.

"Yes, he was a wonderful boy today," Jenna said from the doorway to the kitchen just as Curt arrived there. She had her hair pulled back, and a few strands had escaped to frame her face becomingly. Her cheeks were flushed, presumably from working in a warm kitchen, and she wore a light green apron that brought out the gold flecks in her eyes. She held a large spoon in one hand.

Curt held up a palm toward Sam. "Way to go, Sam! I knew you could do it."

With a brilliant smile, Sam returned Curt's high five. "I even setted the table."

"I noticed that," Curt said.

"Sam, the past tense of *set* is *set,*" Jenna said as she turned to go back into the kitchen.

"I thought you added *e-d* to words to make them past tents," Sam said, trailing after Jenna.

Curt grinned at Sam's slight mispronunciation as he stepped into the kitchen, which was replete with savory cooking smells that had his stomach going nuts.

"Normally you do," Jenna replied. "But in this case, the past-tense form is the same as the present-tense form."

"That's confusing," Sam said, hopping up to look in the bowl as Jenna stirred.

"It sure is," Curt replied, noting the plate of roasted chicken on the counter, flanked by a huge bowl of fresh green beans.

"I agree," Jenna said. "But you have to learn the exceptions to the rules in grammar."

"So, Mr. Graham," Sam said with an effective move to change the subject, "can we do my times tables after dinner?"

Curt looked to Jenna.

"It's fine with me," she said, her eyes on Sam. "Your mom's working late tonight, so you'll have plenty of time before she comes and picks you up."

"Yippee!" Sam crowed before he headed out of the kitchen, already back into floor-sliding mode.

Jenna regarded Curt. "I've never seen him this excited at the prospect of memorizing his times tables." She gave him a lopsided smile. "You certainly have the magic touch."

"I don't know about that," Curt replied. "I'm novel to him, that's all."

"Maybe that's part of it," she said, stirring a pat of butter into the mashed potatoes. "But the other part of it is you're great with him."

Her compliment pleased him; for some reason, having Jenna see him in a good light meant a lot. Maybe because no one had ever had any confidence in him before. Including himself. "I see myself in him." Wild. Unfocused. Precocious.

"Well, I only hope he turns out as well as you did."

Her comment reminded Curt that she didn't know everything about him—only what he'd chosen to reveal to her. If she did eventually find out about his past, she surely wouldn't be doling out compliments. She'd probably be disgusted by his addiction. She might even decide he wasn't an appropriate influence on Sam....

Curt's stomach tensed and for the life of him he couldn't conjure up a response to her statement. He was thankful when Sam barreled back into the kitchen and saved Curt from having to reply.

"Miss Landry is ready for dinner," Sam announced. "Is it time to eat?"

Jenna picked up the bowl of potatoes. "It is," she said. "Go wash your hands, please."

"I'll do the same and we'll meet you in the dining room," Curt said, his throat made tight by thinking about how Jenna might react when she found out the truth about him.

She nodded, then grabbed the green beans and turned toward the dining room. "Sounds like a plan."

Curt followed her out of the kitchen, then continued to the hall bath after she veered into the dining room. As he walked down the hall, hearing the water running as Sam washed up, Curt realized his appetite had vanished, only to be replaced by a looming sense of apprehension and dread.

How in the world would he ever tell Jenna about his drug addiction? His poor choices? All of the things that made his past so complicated?

He had no idea, but knew with certainty that

doing so would be one of the hardest things he'd ever had to face, much less actually do.

And given his checkered past, that was no small potatoes.

From where she stood drying dishes, Jenna watched Curt and Sam, amazed at the scene unfolding before her.

"…and nine times nine is…?" Curt sang in his baritone voice as he strummed along with his guitar.

"Eighty-one!" Sam sang. Sort of; his "singing" was more like shouting.

Nodding in approval, Curt went on with the song. "And seven times six is?"

His face flushed with excitement, Sam replied, "Forty-two!"

And from there, they went back through the times tables randomly, the whole thing a silly song that Curt had made up on the fly.

Who would have guessed that simply putting the multiplication facts to song would be such an effective way to teach Sam?

Curt had figured it out; after dinner, he'd excused himself and gone upstairs, only to return with his guitar. With wide eyes, Sam had been all over the instrument, and all over Curt with questions. How long had Curt been playing? Where did he get the guitar? Was it easy to learn to play?

Curt had answered all of the questions with patience, and once Sam was questioned out, Curt had begun to sing the times tables.

Sam had been entranced. Focused. Eager to learn something she'd had a terrible time even getting him to pay the slightest amount of attention to, much less actually learn. Now she had no doubt he'd never forget what he'd learned in song.

Why hadn't the teacher in her thought of that?

She surreptitiously looked at the two of them, Curt sitting with his guitar across his knee, Sam dancing with excitement next to him, jumping up and down with every correct answer he gave.

Kudos to Curt. He was quite a guy. And Sam adored him.

Something in the vicinity of her chest tightened, leaving her a tad breathless. The feeling was familiar when Curt was around, and she wasn't quite sure what to do about the disconcerting emotions. Ignore them? Pretend they didn't exist? Hope they just went away? Deny, deny, deny?

Or maybe she could just blindfold herself and plug her ears for the next few weeks while Curt lived here. She snorted under her breath. Yeah, as if that was going to work.

Sam wasn't the only one entranced by Curt. Just as she'd been entranced by Garrett, against her better judgment. He'd had warning signs all over him—a terrible childhood, he'd barely managed to graduate high school, sketchy friends, no regular job. But she'd overlooked all of that and had gone with her heart. And it had backfired when she caught him red-handed.

She had to be more careful now.

Troubled by her dilemma, she bit her lip and grabbed the sponge, scratchy side out, and went to work taking out her emotions on a particularly stubborn glob of dried food on the counter. It wouldn't necessarily help her with her predicament, but she'd have the cleanest kitchen counter in town, and that wasn't a bad thing.

With vigor she put some elbow grease into the job—anything to keep her attention away from the endearing scene playing out at her kitchen table.

"Miss Jenna?" Sam said, pulling on her sleeve.

"Oh, um…yes, honey?" she said, her voice high.

"Wow, that counter must really be dirty," Sam said. "You didn't even hear me talking to you."

She put the sponge down and swiped her hair back with her forearm. "There was a nasty spot there." And she'd been so caught up in her quandary about Curt, she'd tuned out. Great. She was using *cleaning* to distract herself from her problems.

"Well, it's gone now," Curt said, giving her an odd look from the table. "In fact, you probably rubbed the finish off."

"I like a clean counter," she said, trying to sound as if manic scrubbing was just part of her normal routine. "Nothing wrong with that."

"Not at all," Curt replied, holding up a hand.

Sam piped in. "Mr. Graham said he would give me a guitar lesson since I did such a good job with my times tables."

She regarded Curt. "Are you sure you have time?"

"I don't have anything else planned for tonight," he replied.

"Well, I do have some of Miss Landry's clothes to put in the wash, so it's okay with me if it's okay with you." Maybe that would get her out of the kitchen, away from the interaction between Curt and Sam. She needed a break from the mushy, off-kilter emotions conjured up by their charming relationship. And, really, she could only scrub so much.

Curt looked right at her, his eyes soft. "You do her laundry?"

She shrugged as she rinsed the sponge out. "It's not included in the room rate, but she has such a hard time doing it herself, I told her I'd help her out." Normally, guests were free to use her facilities to do their own laundry.

"That's very kind of you," Curt said, his eyes searching her face.

She focused on folding the dish towel just so.

"I'd want someone to do the same for Grams," she replied.

"Good point," he said. "But it's still going above and beyond."

"It's the right thing to do."

"And I admire that you think about that." Curt strummed a chord. "You're a good person."

Warmth bloomed in her cheeks. "Thank you." Who would have guessed Curt's approval would mean so much to her? But it did. Oh, it did.

Sam interrupted, "I'm ready to learn to play the guitar."

"Just so you know, bud, it's going to take a while for you to actually learn." Curt patted the chair next to him. "We'll learn one chord tonight, and if you practice some, I'll teach you more another time."

"Awesome!" Sam said, literally jumping into the chair to Curt's side. "I can't wait!"

Ever so gently Curt placed the guitar in Sam's lap and then slid the strap over Sam's narrow shoulders. "I need to tell you how to handle an instrument first."

Sam looked up at Curt, his eyes shining with admiration. "Cool."

Jenna's insides clenched. She had to get away from the sight of the big man and the young boy, bonding over something as simple as a guitar.

"You two go ahead," she said. "I'll be puttering around for a bit."

She quickly left the kitchen, sternly reminding herself that a man with such a complicated past wasn't what she wanted. She scurried into the laundry room and started putting Miss Landry's clothes in the washer, sorting darks and lights as she went. Thankfully, the heartwarming inter-action between Curt and Sam was safely out of sight.

But…definitely not out of mind.

Chapter Ten

"Good job," Curt said. "You just learned the C chord!" He had his arm around Sam, helping him hold his fingers in the right position, but Sam was doing all the strumming himself.

With a gigantic grin, Sam looked at him. "I love the guitar." He strummed again, producing a pretty in-tune C. "Can I learn another chord?"

Curt looked at his watch. "It's getting late, and your mom will be here soon."

Just then, Jenna walked into the kitchen, a laundry basket in hand. She looked at them, and then, with a discreet yet unmistakable shifting of her eyes, seemingly averted her gaze, focusing intently on shifting the laundry basket to her other hip. Odd.

"Miss Jenna!" Sam wiggled in his chair, oblivious to her strange body language. "Look what Mr. Graham taught me."

She set the laundry basket down on the counter, looking as if she took a deep breath as she did so. But the basket missed and fell with a clatter on the tile floor, spilling clothes all over.

"Oh, no." She bent and quickly began gathering up the garments. "I seem to be all thumbs tonight."

Curt unwrapped his arm from around Sam and made to get up and help.

She held up a hand. "No, stay there. I've got this. And I'm pretty sure Miss Landry will be mortified if you handle her unmentionables."

He frowned. "You sure?"

"Positive."

"What are unmentionables?" Sam asked.

Curt bent down and whispered the answer in his ear.

"Oh." Sam thought for a moment. "Why not just say 'underwear'?"

Jenna chuckled. "Good question, Sam."

In no time she had the wayward laundry back in the basket. "No harm done." She turned, her mouth pressed into a very bright smile. "So, Mr. Sam. Are you an expert guitar player now?"

"Yup," Sam replied. "Come see."

As Jenna moved closer to them, Curt took a hold of Sam's hand and guided his fingers into the correct position over the strings. "You got it?"

Sam nodded. "Got it."

"Strum away," Curt told him, trying to ignore Jenna standing right in front of them, bent down slightly, her face alight with interest.

Sam strummed in a semblance of the up, up, down rhythm Curt had taught him.

"Look at you!" Jenna exclaimed, crouching down, resting her arms on her bent knees. "You'll be playing in your own band before long."

"I know," Sam answered, squirming under Curt's arm. Then he abruptly stopped strumming. "Hey, Miss Jenna. I have an idea."

"What's that?" she asked, her gorgeous green eyes focused on Sam.

"Why don't you have Mr. Graham teach you to play guitar, too," Sam said. "Then we could all play together."

Jenna's eyes widened, and then she shot to her feet and literally skittered backward. "Well, um…I don't know…"

Suddenly, teaching Jenna to play sounded like a great idea to Curt. He had a feeling it had something to do with being close to her, but he wouldn't explore that too deeply right now. It just felt right to teach her what he knew. About guitar.

"You need a lesson," Sam said, untangling himself from Curt's arm, then the guitar strap, before shoving the instrument back at Curt. Curt grabbed it before it fell, pushing his chair away.

Free of the guitar, Sam scrambled to his feet,

then reached out and took Jenna's hand, pulling her toward the chair he'd just left. "He's the best-est teacher ever."

"Best." Jenna let herself be pulled toward Curt. Grudgingly, if her stiff posture and slow-as-molasses way of walking was any indication. "Bestest isn't a word, Sam."

Man, she was cute when she put her grammar hat on. With a smile that went clear to his heart, Curt gestured to the chair next to him. "Have a seat, Miss Jenna, and let's get started."

"Yeah, sit." Sam gave her a little push. "If I can play, so can you."

Jenna dropped into the chair. "This lesson could wait until another time." She leaned away and gave Curt an awkward glance as she shoved her hair behind one ear. "I have a lot of things to do."

"You can take a few minutes to do this." Curt held up the guitar. "It'll be fun." Boy, would it. In fact, he couldn't think of anything he wanted to do more than be Jenna's guitar instructor. To enhance her musical knowledge, of course.

She licked her lips, smiled uneasily, and then gingerly took the guitar from him, "O-okay."

Curt scooched his chair a little closer.

Jenna jumped. "What are you doing?"

He pulled in his chin. "Getting closer."

"Why?" she queried with a sideways glance.

Sam piped in with, "So he can help your hand do the chord, silly."

"Right." Curt kept scooching and the chair squeaked on the tile floor. "I need to help position the guitar and show you the hand position."

Jenna nodded quickly. "Oh." She laughed, which came out more like a cute snort. "Okay. Gotcha."

He studied her. "Are you nervous?"

"No," she replied very quickly, in what sounded like a strangled voice, shifting in her seat. "Why would I be?"

"Yeah, why would you be?" Sam said. "'Cause the guitar is easy, Miss Jenna." He patted her shoulder. "If I can learn, you can," he repeated.

"Thank you, Sam, that makes me feel *so* much better," she said in a way that seemed as if she meant exactly the opposite.

She *was* nervous. Obviously so. Interesting. "It's just a guitar lesson," Curt said. "Nothing more."

She nodded. "I know that."

"So just relax and let me do the teaching," Curt said, holding up an arm to indicate he was going to put it around her shoulder. "May I?"

She swallowed visibly. "Y-yes."

He continued, settling his arm around her slender shoulders, his nose coming close to her hair. The scent of her fresh-smelling shampoo wafted his way, filling his senses with the sweet aroma of Jenna.

He resisted his first urge, which was to lean in and breathe deep. Instead, he focused on the fact that her shoulders were stiff and hunched under his arm. He put his hand on her shoulders and shook gently. "You're never going to be able to play if you don't loosen up a bit."

Her frame settled a bit. "Sorry," she murmured.

"Better." He took a hold of her left hand and placed it on the fretboard. Her fingers quivered beneath his. Yeah, she was nervous for sure. "Now I'm going to show you the chord."

He did so, guiding her fingers to the proper places on the frets. She kept her face down, looking at their hands, almost as if she was afraid to look his way. Or maybe she was just really concentrating. Perhaps that was a good thing. More shampoo smell teased his nose. Then again, maybe not....

He cleared his throat. "There, that's the proper position for the chord." He let go. "Do you have it?"

She nodded, just a single upward motion of her head.

"Now strum," he instructed.

Awkwardly, she ran her fingers across the strings over the sound hole. A half-on, half-off C chord emanated from the guitar.

"Wow," she said, strumming again.

He leaned closer, needing to check her finger position.

"It sounds pretty good!" A moment later, she turned, her mouth curved up into a brilliant smile. About six inches from him. She froze, staring into his eyes, clearly surprised to find him so close.

His heart thundered in his chest and he couldn't for the life of himself look away from those beautiful, emerald-shaded eyes of hers. Her left hand dropped from the guitar neck and he roamed his gaze over her smooth, rosy cheeks and delicate eyebrows, landing on her mouth. Instantly he had the insane urge to close the distance between them and kiss her.

"Hey, keep strumming," Sam said, breaking Curt and Jenna's visual connection. "Up, up, down, Miss Jenna."

Jenna blinked, then snapped her gaze away, an unmistakable blush staining her cheeks.

Curt's cheeks were warm, too.

The doorbell rang at that moment.

Jenna's head whipped to her left.

"Yoo-hoo!" a voice called from the foyer.

"Oh, that's your mom," Jenna said, handing Curt the guitar without looking his way. "Guess the lesson's over."

"Oh, no," Sam whined. "I wanted to hear you play more."

"Yeah, me, too," Curt echoed truthfully. He'd liked being her teacher, having her close.

"Sorry," Jenna said, getting to her feet, spending a lot of time smoothing her top down. "It's getting late, and you need to go home and get to bed."

Sam scowled.

"It's a school night." Jenna headed over and grabbed a drinking glass from the counter.

"Can I have another lesson soon?" Sam said, his voice dripping with hope.

Jenna filled the glass with water from the tap and took a big swig. "That's up to Mr. Graham," she said, throwing Curt a brief glance. Up the glass went again. She finished the liquid in one fell swoop, gulping.

Curt pulled his attention from Jenna's body language, which screamed *unsettled*. "Tell you what, bud," he said to Sam. "Miss Jenna and I will talk, and figure out a lesson schedule, okay?"

"Okay!" Sam replied, clapping, his eyes shining in delight.

Jenna pointed toward the foyer. "Um, I'm going to go talk to your mom, Sam." She quickly headed out of the kitchen, then looked back from the kitchen door. "Gather up your things, all right?"

"All right," Sam said.

Jenna left the room.

Curt picked up Sam's backpack and held it

open. "I'm happy to give you more guitar lessons, and help you with your homework, but you have to continue to behave and work on your times tables. And whatever other schoolwork Miss Jenna says you have to do."

Sam put a library book into the open backpack. "I can do that."

Curt shoved a notebook in, then held out a hand. "Let's shake on it."

Sam's small hand shot out and shook Curt's.

"Now we have what's called a gentleman's agreement," Curt told him in a serious tone.

Sam's brow creased. "What's that?"

"It's when two men shake hands and agree, on their honor, to keep a promise."

"Oh, yeah, then," Sam said, nodding. "We have one of those gentleman thingies."

"Excellent," Curt replied. "Miss Jenna works hard, and she needs your cooperation."

"Yeah, I know," Sam said.

Curt picked up the full backpack. "Is that everything?"

"Yup."

"Then put this thing on and head out." Curt held the backpack up.

Sam slipped into it, then turned and abruptly threw his arms around Curt's waist. "Thanks, Mr. Graham. I liked our lesson."

Curt's chest compressed, unfurling tender feelings, the kind he rarely had. "You're welcome," he said, pressing his hands to Sam's narrow shoulders. "And why don't you start calling me Curt."

Sam pulled back. "Miss Jenna says I have to call you Mr. Graham." He rolled his eyes. "She says it's good manners."

Jenna. Miss Manners and Miss Grammar Guru, all rolled into one special package. "Oh, well, then, I guess we'll have to get her approval."

"Cool." Sam threw a glance to the front of the house, and his small shoulders sagged. "I wish I didn't have to leave. I like being here with you and Miss Jenna."

More mushy stuff exploded behind Curt's rib cage, and his throat went thick. He sensed more sincerity in this kid's innocent proclamation than anything he'd ever heard from anyone in his other life.

Or what he was now thinking of as less than half a life. In fact, he realized with sudden clarity, he'd been barely living for a long, long time.

A sense of belonging overcame him, making him feel more at home and happier—more balanced, too—than he'd ever been. "I like you being here, too. But don't you think your mom would miss you if you were here all the time?" Curt would have loved to have that kind of caring when he was a kid. Instead, he'd always felt as if his parents, especially his dad, wouldn't have missed Curt at all if he'd suddenly been gone.

"Well...yeah," Sam said.

Curt put a hand on Sam's neck and gently pushed, encouraging him to start walking toward the foyer.

Jenna returned, looking perplexed. "What are you two doing in here?" She looked at Sam. "C'mon. Your mom is exhausted after a long day at work."

"We were just talking," Curt said, giving her a look as if to say, "We were having a heart-to-heart."

"Ah, I see," she said.

"But we're done now," Curt said.

"Well, then, let's get you out of here, Master Sam, so you and your mom can go home and get to bed."

Curt bade Sam goodbye with an affectionate squeeze to the boy's arm, and then watched him and Jenna walk down the hall toward the foyer.

Jenna shot him a look over her shoulder, with the barest hint of a smile and more of that appealing flush on her pretty cheeks. Then she turned away quickly, her face turning oddly blank, as if she'd seen, or done, something she shouldn't have.

Or *felt* something? For him?

That thought almost knocked him off his feet.

Gathering himself, he went back to the table to get his guitar stuff.

But Jenna's reaction couldn't be ignored so easily. Clearly, she was discombobulated, or something close to it. And so was he. The guitar lesson had become about a lot more than just him teaching her a guitar chord and strumming.

The time they'd spent together sitting side by side on those two kitchen chairs, a guitar between them, his hand on hers, had also been about his and Jenna's attraction. Their eye lock had proven that.

Was the draw he felt to her returned? Did she like him?

His hopes rose, then fell just as quickly. He shook his head. He had to be imagining her "reaction" to him. She was an intelligent, caring, exceptional woman who deserved the best in a man.

And if there was one thing Curt had never been it was the best. Of anything.

Chapter Eleven

Jenna stood back and looked at the walnut stairway railing she'd just polished to a high sheen, wanting to be sure it shined bright enough to see her reflection.

The ladies attending the Moonlight Cove Garden Club tea tomorrow were undoubtedly picky housekeepers from way back. Jenna wanted to impress them in every way possible, be it a high-gloss stair railing or carpet vacuumed to within an inch of its life.

Her tummy did an anxious tumble; tomorrow was an important day. If the ladies in the club liked what she did for them, then they were going to book their monthly meeting at the inn, giving her some much-needed regular business. That in turn would help pay for some of the repairs to the inn.

To that end she'd been cooking and cleaning

since sunup. She'd only taken a break at lunch, and then dinner to serve Miss Landry the crock roast beef and vegetables she had put in at dawn.

Fortunately, Sam was on a school holiday and he and his mom had gone out of town to visit his grandmother in Yakima, so Jenna wouldn't have to take care of him today. Though she loved having him around, it was far easier to prepare for the tea without him underfoot.

She wished she could say the same about Curt's absence. He'd arrived home from work following dinner, and, after eating the foil-covered meal she'd put in the refrigerator for him, had gone up to his room to get his guitar. He was now ensconced on the porch, singing what sounded like a folk song that was vaguely familiar. Something about the answer blowing in the wind?

Which partially explained her cleaning spree; anything to keep herself inside, away from him, would do. She was marginally successful blocking out his mesmerizing voice and haunting guitar playing, though memories of her guitar lesson two nights ago hadn't been as easily kept at bay.

In fact, she'd thought of little else since then.

Now on the bottom step, she worked at a dull spot on the wood, putting her elbow into the job. What had she been thinking, letting herself agree to that lesson? The second his strong arm went around her, she'd been like a piece of bacon left too long in the frying pan. Fried. Her breathing had gone all funny, her fingers had turned fat and clumsy and her senses had gone haywire.

And for the record, whoever had invented the aftershave he wore ought to be hung up by their toes on behalf of unsuspecting women everywhere. No man had the right to smell that good. Just the thought of his scent, all spicy and masculine and wonderful, had her tummy doing backflips worthy of an Olympic gymnast.

And during the lesson, when she'd turned and found him so close to her, she could see just how curly his eyelashes were, how deep his gaze could go, well…she'd almost keeled over right there on the kitchen floor from lack of oxygen and heart palpitations. No doubt about it, Curt had a very disturbing effect on her. Both physically and mentally.

The sight of him bent close to Sam, patiently teaching him to play guitar, the big man tenderly helping the small boy, had made her insides— and knees—liquefy to the point she'd had to put a hand on the wall to steady herself. Covertly, of course. She was getting good at covering up her reactions to him.

Curt was so patient, so caring with Sam, remarkably so, as if it were second nature to him. And the fact that Curt had taken time to help Sam with his homework—and in such an ingenious way, singing the times tables in a fun, creative way—had really made her appreciate him.

Something shifted inside of her, setting all her carefully managed emotions into a tailspin. She paused her robo-polishing motion and put her head down, trying to gain control.

She caught her reflection in the railing—wow, she *had* done a great job polishing it to a sharp luster—her blush obvious, even in an inanimate wooden object.

Flustered, she stepped back, expecting to find the hardwood floor at the base of the stairs. But she found nothing but air. She fell backward, stepping on the bottom step crookedly. Her left ankle joint rolled outward, and white-hot pain exploded and shot up her leg. She managed to land correctly on the bottom step with her right foot, but her momentum carried her backward. She hit the hardwood floor on her backside with a *clump,* letting out a little shriek.

After a moment of silent shock, tears came to her eyes, and she gathered herself enough to grip her left knee as she held that foot off the floor, fighting the urge to scream long and hard at the pain radiating from her ankle in a sharp, pulsing throb.

After a few agonizing moments, she took a second to assess things, mentally going over herself. Even the slight motion made her ankle joint catch fire.

Oh, yeah. She'd definitely done some damage, that much was clear.

No, no, no. She couldn't be hurt; she didn't get sick leave, and tomorrow was a big day. Every day was a big day when you were self-employed.

Trying not to jump the gun, she gulped in air as her tears crested and wet her cheeks. Shaking, her heart punching against her chest wall, she lifted her jeans and looked at her sock-covered left ankle. Her hopes plummeted. Through her sock she could see that the ankle was already puffed and swollen. Her shoe on that foot felt tight, and the pain, oh, the pain…

Stifling a sob, she thought about trying to pull herself up with the stair railing in front of her. But she was pretty sure the injured ankle wouldn't bear the weight. Not in its present injured condition. No way. She needed help. And maybe a doctor.

Fighting down panic, she knew she'd have to get assistance to haul herself off the floor. But how?

Soft guitar playing floated to her from the porch. *Curt.* Curt was here. He could help her. *Thank You, Lord.*

She wiped her cheeks and tried to calm down before she called out to him. She didn't want to unduly alarm him—though her present situation was pretty alarming—so she forced a calm into her voice as she said loudly, "Curt?"

Nothing but music echoed through her.

"Curt?" she shouted, louder this time. Searing pain pounded into the nerve endings in her ankle, and she stifled a groan and cringed.

The music stopped.

"Curt?" she hollered, her head bent, stopping short of an outright bloodcurdling scream.

After a beat of silence she heard a clunk, and a scant three seconds later he came storming through the front door, his face creased with concern. He froze, scowling.

"Jenna!" He rushed over and crouched down. "What happened?"

She sniffed and tried not to cry. "I fell on the stairs."

"Are you hurt?" he asked, putting a warm hand on her bare shoulder next to her tank-top strap. His dark gaze roamed over her, homing in on her foot at the last second.

Nodding, she pointed to her ankle. "I rolled my ankle and think I did something bad to it."

"Okay," he said, getting onto his knees. "Uh… do you want me to look at it?"

"You'd better," she said, her voice cracking. "It really hurts."

He reached out, then hesitated. "Do you want

me to lift you to the couch, or do you want to stay here?"

"Here is fine," she replied, biting her lip. "I'm afraid to move." Not that she doubted he could lift her without any problem. He looked really strong. Capable.

"All right." He paused again, his hands hovering near her ankle.

"Here, let me move my pants leg." She pulled her boot-cut jeans out of the way.

"I'm going to have to take off your shoe and sock," he said, his brow creased. "It might hurt."

"Probably." She took a deep breath. "But we have to get a look at it."

"Right," he replied. "I'll be as gentle as I can."

All she could do was nod. Anxiety hovered on the edges of her control; she had too many responsibilities for an injury. Too many people depending on her.

He managed to get her shoe untied without jarring her ankle, and then with infinite care, went to work removing it. But the motion was excruciating.

A moan escaped from her and she grabbed him, her fingers digging into his firm biceps.

He stopped and pulled his hands away, his lips pressed into a firm line.

She closed her eyes and braced herself. "Go ahead. I can take it."

"Well, I can't," he said, shaking his head. "Seeing you in pain really gets me."

In any other place in time, that sentiment would have meant a lot to her. But with her ankle on fire and a disastrous injury looming, she had other things to worry about. "The shoe has to come off."

Head down, he paused, clearly thinking. After a few moments, he seemed to come to a decision. "Yes. But if your ankle is broken, I might injure it further."

"Okay," she said, starting to feel a bit dizzy from the pain. A broken ankle? How in the world would she manage with that? She wouldn't.

"I don't want to hurt you." He looked right at her, his expression brimming with distress. "I think we should just go to the emergency room without doing anything."

She put a shaky hand on the floor and leaned back, fighting out-and-out panic. "At this point, I'm not arguing."

"Okay, then." He leaned in. "I'll do my best not to make it any worse."

"Quit worrying about me," she said, gritting her teeth.

"That isn't possible," he said solemnly, his eyes meeting hers for the barest of seconds.

Her heart jerked in her chest at his words, but she didn't know what to say. So she remained silent. She just nodded.

In one motion he put his right arm underneath her knees and snaked his left arm behind her. With his face close, he said, "You ready?"

She put her arms around his neck and tightened her grip to steady herself as best she could. "As I'll ever be."

"Okay, then, here we go." With little effort, it seemed, he smoothly got to his feet, cradling her like a baby against his broad, firm chest, as if she were light as a feather. Her leg jostled a bit, and her ankle responded with a thudding, painful protest, firmly reminding Jenna it was injured, but she bit her lip and managed to stifle a groan. She had to buck up and get through this.

God, I need You to help me be strong.

Curt headed for the door, his stride quick and purposeful, his arms gentle but solid around her. She felt safe and cared for, and that put her mind at ease. Kind of; all kinds of apprehensions still peppered her.

How was she going to host the garden club tea if she was laid up with a bum ankle? How would she do anything if she couldn't be up and around?

Halfway to the door, Curt stopped. "Shoot. I have to get my keys upstairs."

"Just put me on the couch," she said from between tight lips, trying to hold her left leg still. "I'll wait there."

He went over and ever so gently set her down on the sofa in the parlor by the front door.

She hissed in a breath as the motion jarred her leg.

"Sorry." He crouched down and took her hand, his eyes soft. "You okay here for a moment?"

"Uh-huh," she replied, blinking back tears, squeezing his hand, hard.

"You want me to carry you up there with me?" He glanced at her ankle, and then back at her face. "I'm not sure I should leave you."

She gave him a trembling smile, or the semblance of one, at least, to put his mind at ease. "No, that isn't necessary." Though his thought was undeniably sweet. And in another set of circumstances his concern would probably have her hoping for things with this man that could never be. Even now, those kinds of wishes swirled in the back of her mind, taunting her with impossibilities. Had to be the shock making her loopy, thinking odd things, wandering to dangerous places.

She had to focus on the here and now, which more than likely had just become dicey beyond belief.

"But I'd do it for you," he said earnestly. "No problem. Whatever you need."

"No," she whispered, touched deeply by his statement. "I'll be fine."

"Okay, then. Just relax for a minute, and I'll be

back." With a nod and a final worried look, he turned and left the room.

She watched him take the stairs two at a time, his long legs eating up the distance. She sat there on the couch, dread spreading as she contemplated how she was going to get along if she'd seriously injured herself.

She did her best not to panic yet, concentrating on trying not to move, hoping concrete thoughts about pain management would keep her anxiety from consuming her. Her ankle throbbed in time with the beating of her heart and, despite her best efforts to stay calm, gnawing worry ate away at her like a giant hungry beast.

To add to her qualms, after seeing Curt in action taking care of her, worrying about her, being there for her when she needed him the most, she couldn't help but long for things that just couldn't be.

Curt held the door to the inn open for Jenna. "Watch the threshold," he said, a funny kind of protectiveness taking over. "Crutches are tricky."

Tentatively she hobbled forward in itsy-bitsy steps, holding her wrapped injured left ankle up. "I don't know if I'm ever going to master these."

"It just takes practice," he said, trying to stand back and let her get the feel of the crutches. Though what he really wanted to do was sweep her off her feet and carry her wherever she wanted to go. "I've had experience with them."

"Oh, yeah, when you had your motorcycle accident."

"Right." He'd been on crutches for months, and had become an expert at getting around on them.

Slowly she made her way over to the couch in the parlor. He followed and took the crutches from her once she was in position to sit. With a sigh she flopped onto the couch.

He set the crutches aside and out of the way, then sat down next to her, his forearms resting on his knees. "What can I get you?"

"A new ankle?"

The E.R. doc had ordered X-rays, which had revealed no fracture. But the swelling and discoloration were, he'd said, indicative of a grade two sprain. He'd wrapped the injured joint, given Jenna a prescription for pain meds, which the hospital pharmacy had filled, and sent her on her way with instructions to keep her foot elevated and to stay off her ankle for the next few days.

Jenna had looked as if she was going to freak out over the diagnosis right there in the E.R.

"I can't help you with a new ankle" Curt said. "But I can help you with anything else you need."

She shifted, wincing, and then went to prop her shoeless, bandage-wrapped left foot on the coffee table. "Wowza, that hurts," she said, grimacing.

Even with eyes swollen from crying and circles of exhaustion marring her cheeks, she looked amazing. But, then, she always did.

Needing to focus on something other than how pretty she was, he said, "Why don't I get you some water and you can take some of the medication the doctor prescribed."

He prayed he was never injured, because he didn't intend to touch that kind of medication again; he knew now it was poison to him, a temptation he could never give in to if he wanted to keep his life under control and on track. Ibuprofen would have to do for any of his aches and pains in the future.

"I'm fine for now," she said. "Aside from being worried about how I'm going to manage around here."

"I'll help you." Just the thought of her struggling and worrying made him want to take on any burden, to make her life easier.

He couldn't remember ever wanting to take care of someone like this before. He'd always put himself first, before others. He cringed inwardly. What an idiot he'd been.

She gave him a shaky smile. "I appreciate the offer, but there's so much to do with the garden club tea tomorrow…" She rested her head against the high back of the couch, as if the weight of her thoughts were too heavy to manage. "And then I have meals to cook for Miss Landry, work to do around here and Sam to take care of on Monday. Not to mention my regular visit to Grams on Sunday." Jenna closed her eyes and pressed her lips together, clearly wrestling to keep control. "And I can't even walk."

He reached out and touched her arm, wanting to offer comfort. "Please don't worry."

Her eyes glittered. "I don't know how I'm going to manage."

"We'll work it out."

"We?" she said, her eyebrows raised.

"Well, yeah." He shifted so he was facing her. "I'm not sure how, but I'll help you get everything done that needs to be done." He wanted to fill the role of caretaker, rather than be the one who needed help.

She smiled, but her lips trembled. "Do you know how to make cucumber tea sandwiches?"

"Well, no." An idea surfaced. "But I know someone who does, or at the very least can figure it out."

"Who?"

"My mom."

A little crease formed between Jenna's eyebrows. "So are you guys getting along?" A valid question, given what Jenna knew of his neglected childhood.

"We talked during the reception, and she asked for my forgiveness." He nodded. "And I gave it."

Jenna gave him a shaky smile. "Hey, that's great."

"Yeah, it is. And I have to say, it feels good to have her back in my life. This could be a good way to bridge the gap between us."

Jenna shook her head. "I still feel funny imposing on her."

"Would you help someone who was injured if you were asked to?"

"Of course."

"Well, then, assume other people will, too."

She chewed on her bottom lip. "I'm not used to asking for help."

"I know. But sometimes God has a plan, and we need to listen." Granted, he was just repeating Marv's words. But now that Curt had found God, the statement meant something to him, sounded right, and he felt comfortable passing along the advice. Another growth point to be proud of.

She took a deep breath, and then let it out. "I'll try."

"Besides, my mom loves to cook, and she loves to boss people around." He grinned. "She'll probably adore taking over."

"I can direct," Jenna said, a hopeful look blooming in her eyes. "With my foot up, of course."

"Oh, yeah, I'm sure you can." He pointed to her crutches. "I can see you waving those things around, telling people what to do."

"Hey, good idea," she said with a grin.

"Oh, boy." He rolled his eyes teasingly. "You might abuse your power now that you have a way to make sure everyone does your bidding."

She wagged her eyebrows. "You've figured out my plan."

"I'm onto you for sure," he said, taking her hand in his, liking the feel of her skin against his own.

Jenna paused, then grasped his fingers. "Thank you so much for taking care of me tonight." She pivoted slightly so she was facing him, her head resting on the back of the couch. "I honestly don't know what I would have done without you."

He stared into her beautiful green eyes, falling into them. "I'm just glad I was here."

"Me, too," she whispered, holding his gaze.

He wanted to kiss her then, as he'd never wanted anything else, and he actually moved a bit toward her before stopping short. Now wasn't the time for that. She was injured. Exhausted. Struggling with how she was going to cope. Vulnerable. It would be wrong to make advances now. And he desperately wanted to do the right thing for once in his life. By Jenna in particular.

So, with effort, he looked away and let go of her hand, pulling his thoughts from the need to take her in his arms and close the distance between them. "Why don't I get you upstairs so we can both get some sleep."

"Okay," she said breathily.

He busied himself helping her stand and get her crutches situated. His mind stuck on his musings of just moments before. For once, he wanted to make the right decisions, to think things through instead of plowing ahead without a thought for the consequences. He was beginning to see he deserved that much, and so did the extraordinary woman beside him.

But…did his need to help her indicate that his feelings for her had veered into dangerous territory? A place that might lead to pain? What if he fell for her, only to have her bear out that she could never return his feelings? Never love a man with his rocky past?

That might break his heart.

And he'd never been good at dealing with the setbacks and trials of life. He'd always let drugs numb him so worry was only a distant echo in his mind, easily ignored and put off. But now that he was clean, he didn't have that crutch anymore. He'd be on his own, with his own vulnerabilities at play, and nothing to help him deal.

A bolt of worry ripped through him, setting his nerves on a crazy edge. He'd have to think about all of those possibilities, outcomes and worries. Later. When he wasn't in the middle of helping Jenna through a medical crisis or rife with the need to coddle her and take care of her every wish.

He wasn't exactly objective right now. And if

there was one thing he'd learned from Marv it was the need to make careful choices and decisions.

Even though pulling away and doing the careful thing made his arms feel emptier than they ever had.

Chapter Twelve

On her crutches, Jenna hobbled onto the patio, where the garden club tea was taking place. She was pleased to see that everything was going as planned.

Ten ladies, all wearing some kind of flower-trimmed hat—a club tradition for many years—sat at one long rectangular table, enjoying their meal of tea sandwiches, sweet scones and home-made jam made with Grams's recipe. The whole affair was rounded out with fresh fruit and a savory assortment of cheese and crackers.

"Jenna, dear, I have to tell you you've done an excellent job with this tea," Mrs. Lofty, the social director of the garden club said, taking off her glasses. "How in the world did you manage this whole thing with your injury?"

"I have Curt Graham and his mother to thank for helping me today," Jenna replied. Mrs. Graham had arrived very early that morning, and had instantly gone to work getting everything ready. Curt had helped her until he'd had to go to work, and then Rose and Benny Kincaid, Kim's aunt and uncle, had arrived to help, too. Jenna was truly overwhelmed by their support.

"Well, you've all done a wonderful job."

Jenna breathed a sweet sigh of relief. "Thank you." Curt had been a godsend last night and this morning taking care of her, and she didn't know how she would have managed without him.

He was honestly one of the most considerate men she'd ever met. She'd never felt more cared for. Or special.

Hoo boy. Feeling the need to do something to keep mushy thoughts of Curt at bay, she slowly negotiated her way over to the beverage station to check on the water pitcher, ignoring the throbbing in her ankle. She might be laid up, but she was determined not to be totally useless.

Although, if from her post in the kitchen Mrs. Graham spotted Jenna up and about, Curt's mom would probably tsk-tsk and give Jenna a stern talking-to. In the nicest way possible, of course. Mrs. Graham had turned out to be gracious and kind, which, given Curt's tales of his neglected childhood, had kind of surprised Jenna. Clearly, his mom had made some changes for the better in her life. Jenna was glad for her. And Curt.

Just as Jenna got to the table set with various pitchers, napkins and an ice bucket, a snippet of conversation snagged her attention.

"...*that* Curt Graham?"

Jenna froze, her ears perked.

"Yes, *that* one," someone said, her voice laced with what sounded like outright disgust.

Jenna's gaze flew to the two ladies sitting closest to the beverage station, their backs to her. She recognized them as Mrs. Leahy and Mrs. Frost.

Mrs. Leahy continued on, "He ran wild when he was younger, and was infamous for causing trouble."

"Wasn't he arrested at one point?" Mrs. Frost asked.

Jenna's jaw went slack.

"Oh, yes. He had numerous run-ins with the law," Mrs. Leahy said, her lip curled. "DUI, reckless driving. My Harold's brother worked for the sheriff's office back then, and he told us some stories about Curt that would curl your hair."

With her crutches each tucked under an armpit, Jenna fiddled awkwardly with one of the pitchers.

"Yes, I remember now," Mrs. Frost said. "My best friend's son knew him in high school, and she used to tell me some of the things Curt did." She made a derisive sound. "Curt Graham was bad news. I remember now that he ended up in the hospital after a motorcycle accident."

"He was drunk." Mrs. Leahy sniffed. "He's a bad egg, to be sure."

Jenna's knees went weak with shock, and she was glad she was held up with the crutches. Arrests? DUI? Curt? No way.

"Heaven help any woman who chooses to get involved with him," Mrs. Frost said as she sipped her tea.

"I was just thinking the same thing," Mrs. Leahy replied with her nose in the air.

Staggered, Jenna stood there for a moment. What should she do? On the one hand, she wanted to defend Curt to the gossipy women; the picture they painted just didn't fit with the man she'd gotten to know. But on the other, some of what they said fit with things Curt had shared with her about his accident and his and his dad's estrangement.

And how could Jenna forget what had happened with Mrs. Woolsey at the wedding reception? Why, the woman had scornfully called him out about his past actions right there on the patio, in front of everybody. Plus, Jenna always felt he'd been holding back, even when he spoke to her about his past. All of that pointed to the veracity of the ladies' story.

Indecision had her fidgeting. Automatically she shifted on her feet and put weight on her ankle. She winced and hunched her shoulders, letting out a little gasp of pain.

A gentle hand touched her arm, startling her out of her swirling thoughts.

"Jenna, dear, are you all right?"

Jenna awkwardly turned and found Rose standing next to her, her brow creased. "Um…yes, I guess." But she wasn't. This was what she got for listening in on others' conversations. Rose's blue eyes went to Jenna's ankle. "Is your ankle bothering you? Maybe you've overdone it."

"Yes, actually, I think I have," Jenna said, feeling suddenly beleaguered by what she'd heard, as if all of her energy had been sucked out of her, leaving her hollow and empty. And hurting in more places than just her bunged-up ankle.

"Why don't you go in and put that ankle up." Rose gestured to the beverage table. "I'll take care of this."

"Thank you, Rose," Jenna replied, adjusting the crutches beneath her arms. "I'm…exhausted." Disillusioned, too. Together, those two things dragged her down and made her feel as if she needed to sit.

"Do you need help?" Rose asked, smoothing back her gray hair into the bun she wore.

"No, no, I can make it on my own." Gingerly Jenna started making her way inside; thank goodness she'd gotten the hang of the crutches. Once she was in the house, she bypassed the kitchen, instinctively wanting to avoid seeing Mrs. Graham just now; Jenna was certain her distress showed, and she didn't want to have to explain why to Curt's mom.

By the time Jenna had hobbled to the couch, her whole ankle burned. Cringing, she propped it up on a pillow and settled back, her thoughts awhirl.

Was what those women said about Curt true?

Uncertainty warred within her. She wanted to chalk up their talk as just malicious gossip between two old ladies who had nothing better to do than trade cruel tittle-tattle. But...she'd heard what she'd heard, and the seeds had been planted. And it all jibed with other things she knew about Curt's past.

She closed her eyes as qualms about him wrapped themselves around her. One question in particular burned within.

Why did she care so much about Curt's past?

She dropped her head into her hands. Unfortunately, the answer to her question was too frightening to even consider. Though she knew she would have to face reality eventually.

She thought back to last night, to the moment when she was sure he'd wanted to kiss her. And how she'd wanted that very thing more than her next breath. How disappointed she'd been when he'd pulled away, as if she'd missed out on something special.

Now she would never know what his kiss would

feel like. She couldn't allow herself to really fall for Curt, not if she wanted the perfect love she'd always dreamed about.

She could only do one thing—she had to guard her heart and not allow any thoughts of what she was missing out on enter her mind.

She just hoped she was strong enough to stick to that decision.

Jenna hobbled down the upstairs hall next to Curt. "Thank you for helping me put together this impromptu potluck for your mom, Rose and Benny. I thought it'd be a good way of thanking them for helping out at the tea."

"No problem. And great news that the inn is now the official meeting place for the garden club," he said.

"Yes, it is," she said, her gaze skating away.

In fact, she hadn't looked directly at him since he'd arrived home from work and taken her to see Grams as they'd planned earlier that morning. In the car, Jenna had seemed distant. Distracted. Quiet. Actually, she didn't seem herself at all, almost as if something had happened at the tea. "You did all the work. We just came in at the end and helped with final details."

"Well, maybe so. But I'm still really grateful to all of you for helping me out."

"It felt good to be needed." Thinking about

others, and not just himself, had healed some of his wounds and had confirmed what the Bible said about putting others' needs before his own.

"Well, I'm grateful. And that you were able to take me to see Grams." Jenna stopped at the top of the stairs, her weight on her good ankle. "I was really worried about how I was going to get over to see her today. I wouldn't have made it there without you."

"I know how much it means to you to see her. I'm glad I could help out." It had made his heart glow to see Jenna and her grandmother together, to witness the love and devotion they shared. The connection between the two Flaherty women was obvious.

And it had made him long for familial relationships of his own. Another goal to work toward, another wish for his future. Maybe he would have a normal life someday. A life like Jenna's.

Tentatively, Jenna put her crutches on the second step down. She paused, half down, half up, her brow furrowed in concentration.

Curt let her go, trying to do as she'd asked and let her be.

The crutches wobbled then steadied, and she transferred her weight from the higher stair to the lower one while holding up her left foot, unbalanced in the narrow step space. All of a sudden she pitched forward, emitting a frightened squeak.

Gasping loudly, Curt put his arms around her to keep her from falling. She sagged against him, breathing fast, her heartbeat thundering against his arm as he pulled her close, safe and sound. Her crutches clattered to the floor and then slid down the wooden stairs.

"I've got you," he said against her ear, tightening his hold. He fought the urge to breathe in deep the fresh citrus-tinged scent of her hair but lost the battle. He shut his eyes, letting himself enjoy her closeness for the briefest of seconds.

She grabbed on to his forearms with her hands. "I'll never master these stairs," she said, her voice breathy. "They're just too steep."

"You don't need to," he said. "I'll carry you." He'd do anything she asked if it would keep her safe. He put one hand under her knees while he slid the other under her arms. "Get ready, Miss Flaherty. I'm picking you up, no arguing." And then he did exactly that, lifting her against his chest, mindful of her injured ankle.

She gave a shriek. "Whoa!"

He settled her into his arms. "No screaming. You'll scare Miss Landry." He looked down at Jenna, loving the up-close view, and the way she fit perfectly against him. He could get used to having her in his arms.

"My, you're pushy," she said, grabbing a hold of his shoulders, her body rigid.

"When it comes to your safety, yes." He headed down the stairs, tempted to take them very, very slowly to prolong the exquisite torture of holding her close. "I don't want anything else to happen to you."

After a pause, she discernibly relaxed. "I appreciate your concern," she said with quiet sincerity. "I guess I'm not used to other people taking care of me."

He reached the bottom of the stairs, but he wasn't in any hurry to put her down. "You take care of everyone else."

"I guess so."

He shifted her up a bit, then looked right at her. "I know so. Miss Landry. Sam. Grams. Me. You take care of all of us, and you never seem to ask for anything in return."

"Well, Miss Landry *is* paying me."

"You know what I mean. You do her laundry, make her special food, keep her company. All of those above-and-beyond things. She isn't paying you for that."

"It just seems like the right thing to do."

"And that's important to you, isn't it?" he asked as a rhetorical observation. Her intrinsic need to help others was one of the things he liked most about her.

"Yes, it is," she said, finally meeting his gaze,

her face closer than it had ever been. Her lips so near he could almost feel them on his.

Spurred by that thought, without thinking much, he dipped his head and kissed her.

For the most sublime second she kissed him back, her mouth soft and sweet, and he felt as if he'd found something he'd been looking for his whole life.

But then, with a tiny groan, she pulled away, pressing her hands against him. "No, no. I can't do this." She squirmed. "Please put me down."

An arrow of disappointment pierced him, but he instantly complied with her request. The last thing he wanted was to make her uneasy. Or force his attentions on her. "Of course." With infinite care, he set her on her feet, keeping a hold of her until she got her one-footed balance, feeling her tremble beneath his touch.

"Thanks," she said in a low, husky voice.

Needing a distraction, he bent down and retrieved her crutches. "Here."

She took them and got them settled in the right place under her arms, never meeting his gaze. A blush stained her cheeks as she hobbled back a bit, creating distance.

That spoke louder than words. He'd messed up, upset her, and that was the last thing he'd meant to do. "I'm sorry," he said. "It's just that…I got the impression you were okay with me kissing you."

She swallowed, nodding. "I was. You didn't do anything wrong."

"Then why—"

"Did I pull away?"

He nodded, putting his hands in his pockets to keep from touching her.

"Because in that moment, with you so close, I couldn't think straight, and I did want you to kiss me."

"But only for a moment?" he said, desperately trying to keep any shade of bitterness from his voice. Her odd manner this afternoon poked at him. What was wrong?

She bit her lip, then smoothed one side of her hair back behind one ear, tilting her head.

She sighed. "I need to level with you, all right?"

"All right," he said, anxiety crowding his chest.

She paused, clearly gathering herself. "I heard some ladies talking about you at the tea, and they said some…things that really…surprised me."

A ball of dread almost choked him. "What kind of things?"

"Things that you did in the past."

"Such as?" he asked, his lips as stiff as stone.

"Such as how you were arrested for DUI and reckless driving." She drew in a shaky breath. "How much trouble you were in when you lived here."

Words stuck in his throat and he found his gaze

glued to the floor. Shame gushed through him in a hot geyser, burning a path in his gut.

She tottered closer, her crutches clunking on the wooden floor. "I wanted to put everything they said aside as just malicious gossip. I wanted to defend you."

"But you didn't," he intoned, his jaw barely moving. And why should she? Everything those women had said was true. Every single word.

"No, I didn't because…" Her eyes suddenly filled with tears.

Her gathering tears killed him. "No, you don't have to explain. I don't want you to have one moment of regret over what happened."

Moisture spilled over and tumbled down her cheeks. "I need to tell you why."

"Okay. Whatever you want." Funny how important her needs had become to him. Maybe that was a good sign for his recovery. Or maybe it just meant he'd let himself care too much for her.…

"I've sensed that you've been hiding something, and I thought maybe this…stuff they talked about…was it."

His throat went dry. "You're very perceptive."

"So, is it all true?" she asked in a bare whisper. In the periphery of his vision he saw her wring her hands in front of herself.

He steeled himself to make the admission. "Yes, yes, it is." He'd never wished more that he could say those ladies' tales of his wild, misspent youth were pure gossip, based on nothing more than untruths and rumor. But he couldn't.

Stiffly, she nodded, and it was as if she'd put a mask in place.

The bottom dropped out of his stomach.

"Thank you for being honest," she said, her voice very even.

He paused, not quite sure what to say. He hated the wall that had crept up between them. He should have been honest with her from the start. Although, when was a good time to tell someone that you'd done terrible things in your youth, that you'd made mistakes and taken the wrong path more times than you could count?

"I think the kiss was a mistake," she whispered.

A mistake. The words cut a wound in his heart. "Because of my past?"

She blinked. "Partly."

"What's the other part?"

"As I told you, I was in love once, and he seemed like a dream come true. But he wasn't." She wiped her cheeks. "He cheated on me and… well, it broke my heart. I have to be careful, take things slow, before I take another chance."

"Your checklist." He fought the urge to add a derisive pitch to his words.

"Miss Landry was exaggerating."

"But you have things you want in a man, and in the here and now, I'm not it."

"I…I'm not sure, but…" She gave a slow back-and-forth motion of her head as more tears wet her cheeks. "Probably not."

He nodded, doing his best to ignore the ripping sensation that slashed through his chest. But he drew himself up, determined not to let her see how much she'd saddened him. "You're entitled to all of that," he said, trying to sound normal. "You're a wonderful person, Jenna, one who deserves the absolute best in life." And in her eyes right now, that wasn't him.

"Thank you for understanding." She sucked in a large, shaky breath. "I…have to get to my guests." Without another word she turned, her head bent, and slowly clumped toward the kitchen.

He forced himself to watch her go. The truth taunted him. He wasn't the man she wanted. He'd made mistakes, and now he was paying for them in a way that cut to the bone. Seemed fitting. Even if that reality made him feel more miserable than he'd been in, well…forever.

Chapter Thirteen

❧

Jenna went through the motions of hosting the potluck, with beverages and dessert provided by her, but her heart wasn't in the festivities.

Jenna, Curt, Benny, Rose, Miss Landry and Mrs. Graham—oh, yeah, she'd asked Jenna to call her Marie—all sat around the dining room table as they ate. Everyone, save for Jenna and Curt, had been talking up a storm about everything from the weather to the upcoming holiday season.

Curt hadn't said a word, smiled or eaten much, and certainly hadn't so much as looked at Jenna since their revealing discussion at the bottom of the stairs. And Jenna had kept quiet, too, her thoughts roiling.

All she could think about was that kiss.

And the shaken look on Curt's face when she'd said the kiss was a mistake, that he more than likely wasn't the man she wanted, and why.

And the sinking feeling that had gripped her when he'd confirmed everything those tea ladies had said was true.

Then again, there was that kiss, which in truth had shaken her to the core.

Her cheeks heated. She made a big show of taking a drink of water, hoping nobody noticed her blush. The evening couldn't end fast enough for her. Sitting here with Curt, surrounded by others, was torture. She wanted to explain herself more to him, ease the sting of what she'd said. Although she wasn't sure any explanation would wipe the hangdog expression from his face. Or ease the hurt she'd caused him.

But, man, had that kiss thrown her. Scared the stuffing out of her with its intensity and its implications. Made her realize how much she liked Curt, despite what those women had revealed.

"You're awfully quiet, Jenna dear," Marie said from her spot to the left of Jenna. "Penny for your thoughts."

Gracious. What could Jenna tell her? *Oh, yes, your son and I kissed just a half hour ago, it sent me spinning, and I freaked out and told him it was a mistake and, man, did it hurt his feelings.*

Um…no. Jenna took another sip of water as she scrambled for a response, latching on to one of the subjects of the recent dinnertime conversation. "Uh, I was just thinking about how much I'm looking forward to the holidays." Sounded plausible. Except, as the words left her mouth, Jenna realized with shock that she wasn't really looking forward to Thanksgiving or Christmas, which were usually her two favorite holidays.

She wadded up the paper napkin in her lap, her fingers clenched.

"Oh, yes, won't it be wonderful?" Marie said. "Especially now that I have grandkids to spoil."

"Oh, that's right. Seth and Kim had a baby not too long ago, didn't they?"

"Yes, they did. A girl named Charlotte, Charlie for short." Marie pulled her cell phone from her pocket. "Would you like to see pictures of her and Dylan?"

Jenna looked over to where Curt sat across the table from her. For the first time since they'd sat down, his dark gaze met hers and held.

Her heart beat a fast tattoo against her chest. "Of course," Jenna managed to say, dragging her eyes away from his stare, glad for a distraction from his perusal. Besides, no one in their right mind refused to look at a doting grandma's photos of her grandkids.

Marie brought up the photos on her cell phone, and Jenna oohed and aahed appropriately; the kids, of course, were adorable, so her reaction wasn't a stretch. Rose, who sat on the other side of Marie, turned her attention to the photos, a smile on her face. Given Rose was Kim's aunt, she spent a lot of time with the kids, and clearly adored them.

A pang hit Jenna when she saw a shot of Seth, Kim, Dylan and Charlie on the beach, with a white-capped ocean at their backs and a blue, blue sky dotted with white clouds stretched above them. Seth, who strongly resembled Curt, held baby Charlie close against his broad chest with one arm, his other around Kim, hugging her close, his lips buried in her dark hair. Blond Dylan, who looked to be about seven or eight, kneeled in the sand in front of them, his arms around a big white poodle with coal-black eyes and curly fur.

Clearly, Seth was deeply in love with Kim, and she with him. And, goodness me, they looked like a deliriously happy family.

Family. A sharp pang of longing stabbed its way into Jenna. She wanted what they had. Wanted love and devotion, and the kind of happiness so clearly illustrated in the photo of the Graham family on the beach. She wanted a man to love her the way Seth loved Kim, with his whole heart and soul.

She'd thought Garrett was the answer to that dream. But he hadn't been the man she'd thought he was. He'd broken her heart, made her wary. Picky. But was she letting past experience have too much power?

She turned to Curt again.

But he was looking up and behind her, to the entryway into the dining room. "Dad," he said, his voice holding an edge of surprised shock. "What are you doing here?"

In concert, Jenna and Marie turned to the doorway behind them.

Curt's dad stood there with ill-fitting clothes, his short gray hair on end and his sunburned face pressed into a scowl that, to Jenna, seemed permanent. He didn't seem like a very happy person. And, according to Curt, he wasn't.

"I have a bone to pick with you," Mr. Graham said, pointing a rigid finger at Curt, his squinty eyes shooting darts.

"Joe, what is this about?" Marie asked.

"Stay out of this, Marie," Mr. Graham barked, glaring at her.

"Hey," Curt said. "Keep your voice down, Dad. And don't talk to Mom that way."

Mr. Graham shot his razor-sharp gaze back to Curt. "You came by my house a few days ago when I was fishing, didn't you?"

Curt slowly put his napkin down. "Yes, I told you I needed to borrow your car-wash supplies so I could wash Miss Landry's car."

Jenna remembered how sweet she thought it had been for Curt to do that. Miss Landry had been thrilled. She'd told Jenna again what a great man she thought Curt was. Jenna had agreed.

"Yes," Miss Landry said. "And he did a wonderful job."

"I'm sure he did," Mr. Graham said, having the good grace to soften his voice a bit when speaking to Miss Landry. Maybe he did have some manners underneath his abrasive exterior.

"Dad, clearly you're upset." Curt stood up, his jaw tensed noticeably. "Why don't you tell us why you're here."

"Something was stolen from my house that day, and I'm thinking maybe you had something to do with it," Mr. Graham said.

"Let me get this straight." Curt stalked around the table. "You think I *stole* something from your house?" His tone reflected downright incredulity. And deep hurt.

Jenna's dander rose. But out of consideration for her elders, she had to forcibly keep herself from ordering Mr. Graham from her house. Along the same lines, the sentiment so clear in the tenor of Curt's query had her wondering if Mr. Graham's brief bout of manners was nothing but a false impression.

Poor Curt. And Marie.

"Yes, that's why I'm here," Mr. Graham groused.

Marie rose abruptly, throwing her napkin down on the table. Her silverware clanked. "Why in the world would your own son steal something from you?" she asked, putting her hands on her hips.

"Yeah," Curt put in, speaking carefully. "Why would I steal from you?"

"Because it was pain medication that went missing," Mr. Graham replied, his eyebrows yanked together. "A whole bottle of the stuff, prescribed to me after I threw my back out a few months ago."

Curt's face twisted and his shoulders sagged, but he stayed silent.

"You think Curt stole your pain meds?" Marie questioned, her voice rising. "Why would he do that, Joe?"

"Because we all know he was addicted to the stuff for years," Mr. Graham snapped. "That's why."

Shock rolled through Jenna and she gaped, her jaw dead slack. She instantly swung her gaze to Curt, her eyebrows raised. He stared at her for a long silent moment. And she saw in the depths of his regret-tinged dark eyes that his dad had spoken the truth.

Though she knew in her heart Curt hadn't stolen his dad's pills, he *had* been addicted to pain meds.

A chill spread through her. She'd just discovered the last bit of what he'd been holding back.

And the revelation hit home that *complicated* didn't even begin to describe his past.

For the first time in a long time, playing his guitar on the porch didn't do a thing to calm Curt down or relax him. Little wonder, what with Dad crashing the potluck and accusing Curt of stealing his pain meds just a few hours earlier.

Curt's gut hollowed out. Things had always been rocky and tense between him and his father, but the man's accusation brought new meaning to the word *dysfunctional.* No doubt about it, his dad had always been quick to jump to conclusions. Even so, this latest episode seemed to be a new low for him.

Curt's wishes for some semblance of a family reconciliation had crashed and burned in the dining room tonight, with Jenna there to witness the whole thing.

A lot of hopes had gone down in flames tonight.

Curt thought back on the look he'd seen on her face when she'd figured it all out—the whole shameful mess of Curt's addiction, announced by his own *father,* no less.

Instantly, the E chord Curt was going for twanged crookedly out of tune. He stopped playing and dropped his head, his eyes closed, his throat thick.

Jenna's obvious shock had been the bitter icing

on top of the evening. He'd known he cared about her—her reaction to their kiss had gutted him, and that had shown him the truth of his feelings—but seeing her astonishment over his past wrongdoings had shoved the fillet knife in even farther.

He let out a little groan.

At least he could be grateful that his mother had calmed his dad down after his pronouncement that he thought his own son was a drug thief, and had hustled him out of the house before Curt could fly off the handle. Bless her for that; Jenna's opinion of him would have sunk even lower if Curt had actually said any of the things that had come to mind when it became clear why his dad was there.

Though, could her opinion of him go any lower? The thought of that reality bothered him. He wanted Jenna's approval. Wanted her to think of him as a good man in heart and action. More than almost anything else he'd ever craved.

Again, regret for his squandered youth blazed through him, making him wish he could turn back time, do things right. Make him worthy of a woman like Jenna.

But Curt had no option but to deal with the bad choices he'd made. He'd just never really understood what that meant until he'd met Jenna.

Until it had been made clear what price he'd pay for the things he'd done.

The party had broken up right after his parents

left, and Rose had given him a big hug and told him to keep his chin up. As Curt thanked her, he'd seen Jenna carefully get to her feet, motion Benny over and whisper something in his ear. He'd nodded and the two of them had disappeared, Benny walking by her side, and when he'd returned alone just a few minutes later, Curt deduced that Benny had helped her upstairs to her room. Curt hadn't seen her since.

Apparently she couldn't even bear to be in the same room with him.

Another shaft of pain splintered through him in the vicinity of his heart.

"I haven't heard my favorite song yet." Jenna's voice, soft and low, came from the shadowy spot by the front door.

His fingers froze on the fretboard and his heartbeat sped up into triple time. "Which one is that?" he managed to say.

"'Michael Row the Boat Ashore,'" she said, materializing out of the dark with little clumping sounds from her crutches. She wore her pink robe and fuzzy slippers, and she had her hair up in a soft bun atop her head. She'd never looked more lovely.

He swallowed. "Guess you've mastered the stairs."

"Yeah, with practice." She shifted the crutches under her arms. "I'd like to hear that song."

"I'm not sure I can play it."

With a frown, she said, "I've heard you play it before."

"I know how," he replied in an even voice. "But my fingers seem to be out of tune tonight."

She stopped at the end of the porch swing and put one hand on the chain. "Why?"

He strummed a random chord, careful to look at his guitar rather than her. "I'm not sure." Not exactly the truth. She was the reason nothing worked. Oh, man. How had he let himself fall for her?

She paused and the silence of the evening echoed between them, broken only by the sound of the frogs croaking in the distance. Finally, she said, "You're upset."

He wasn't going to lie. "Yes, I am. My dad and I have never seen eye to eye, and we've had plenty of verbal skirmishes and disagreements, but what he did…" Curt shook his head. "It really hurt." Of course, he was troubled by her reaction to the revelation of his addiction, too. But he wouldn't go into that. He didn't want to put her on the spot, or make her have to defend herself in any way. Her reaction was completely valid.

Plus, just the thought of discussing his addiction with her made him sweat.

Carefully she maneuvered herself over and sat down next to him, putting her crutches on the floor underneath the swing. She then folded her hands demurely in her lap. "Do you want to talk about what he said?"

Curt let out a rough breath. "Not really." Though Marv would quickly set Curt straight about the error of the clam-up strategy.

She nodded, her gaze on her knees. "I figured you'd say that."

All he could do was shrug. He was nothing if not predictable when it came to discussing difficult things.

"Well, I'd like to talk about it, if you don't mind."

He shuddered; telling her about his shameful past would be difficult. He wasn't sure he was strong enough to do it. "I'm not big on talking about what happened." His first instinct had always been to fold inward and avoid opening up.

"How has that worked for you?" she asked.

He inclined his head. Touché. "Not very well." In fact, that strategy had propelled him to keep others on the periphery while he wasted his life on drugs and shallow relationships that left him feeling empty and alone.

He was determined to change that pattern. That was why he'd moved back to Moonlight Cove. Why he'd sought to rebuild familial relationships and find a balanced way of living. Why he wanted a new life.

"So maybe you should try a new strategy," she said.

"You sound like my recovery counselor." Marv had actually said that to him many times, and had made Curt much more aware of adjusting to life's ups and downs.

"You have a counselor?" she asked.

"Yes, I had one at the rehab center I went to."

"Drug rehab, I take it?" she said in a level voice.

"Yes," he replied under his breath. "I've been clean and sober for six months now."

"Hey, that's great," she said. "You have a lot to be proud of."

"I do." He shifted uneasily, and then set his guitar aside. "But…I have a lot to be ashamed of, too. And lots of regrets."

She was silent for a moment. "Everyone has stuff in their past that they regret."

"I know. But when I look back on the bad things I did, I shudder." He thinned his lips. "I was messed up, and didn't have a clue how to behave."

"I've gathered your parents weren't the greatest role models."

A snort escaped. "No, they weren't. I look back now and realize that I did a lot of stuff back then just to get their attention."

"And it didn't work?"

"Nope." No matter what he did, all he got from

his dad was guilt. His mom hadn't doled out guilt. But she hadn't given support, either. She'd been too caught up in marital problems, Curt supposed. She was always in her room, upset, licking her wounds from the latest bout with his dad. Curt had always wondered how she could be *there* physically but not really be present.

At least she was here now.

"You said you and your dad had a falling-out after your motorcycle accident?" Jenna adjusted herself on the swing and it shifted Curt's way a bit. "What happened there?"

He felt his walls rise but he pushed them down. He had to open up to her for himself and as part of his path to recovery.

Curt forged ahead. "I was drunk that night, and on the way home from a party at a friend's house, I crashed my motorcycle into a tree out on Old Ridge Lane," he blurted, needing the truth out, once and for all. Hopefully, confessing his sins to her would be cathartic.

Jenna said nothing, clearly waiting for him to continue.

He did so. "As I told you, I broke a vertebra, messed up my spine, broke a few ribs and my leg."

"Yes, I remember," she said in an even tone.

"I was a mess. Spent a week in the hospital. My dad came to visit me once, the day I was to be released."

She gasped. "You were in the hospital after a serious accident, and he only came to visit you once?"

"That was the way he rolled."

"I…just can't imagine that."

"I don't have to imagine it." Curt leaned forward and rested his forearms on his thighs. "It happened for real."

"I am so sorry."

Something occurred to him. He turned and looked at her. "I'm not telling you all this for your sympathy." Absolutely true. And that attitude signaled a turning point for him. In the past, he'd always been the king of excuses, rationalizations and stories, all told to garner sympathy from others, and also to diminish the ugly truth of his behavior in his own conscience.

Maybe he was on the course to changing his ways for good. Hope rose.

After a pregnant pause, she said, "Why *are* you telling me this?"

"I'm telling you because I see now that I need to for my recovery."

"Fair enough," she said.

"Anyway, my dad visited me. He came into my room and announced that he'd talked to the police and gotten the dirty details about my accident, and that seeing as how I was now a drunk with a DUI, I was no longer welcome in his home." A spasm moved through Curt, sharp and strong. "I lost so much that night. My life as I knew it. My self-respect. My dad. All of it was gone."

"How old were you?" she asked.

"Barely eighteen." He scoffed, "An adult in my parents' eyes."

"Oh, no." A pause. "What did you do?"

"I took the hundred bucks he gave me for bus fare to wherever and moved in with a friend's family while I recovered."

"That had to be rough, having your dad do that."

"Yeah, it was," he replied, barely moving his lips. "It was the final nail in the coffin of our relationship."

She shook her head, her eyes reflecting shock. "What happened after that?"

Curt shifted, stretching his tense neck muscles. "I was prescribed pain meds after my accident, and I took them as prescribed. My injuries were pretty bad, so I needed them for about six months."

"Go on," she said softly.

"I'd moved to California to play in a buddy's band." He closed his eyes for a moment. "I tried to get off those pain meds, I really did. But by that time I was hooked, and every time I tried to quit taking them, I'd get deathly ill, like I had the worst flu ever."

He scrubbed a hand across his face. "I was clueless, and I was just trying to survive down there in L.A. I kept taking them—the docs kept giving them to me because of the extent of my injuries—and after a while, I was flat-out dependent on the meds. I went to rehab a few times, but it never stuck." He grimaced. "Until six months ago. That's when everything changed."

"What happened?"

He didn't want to tell her, didn't want to see the scorn in her eyes. But he had to.

He swallowed and pushed on. "I went to a party after a gig, drank too much and took too many pills." He hung his head, never feeling more ashamed. "I overdosed, and the E.R. doc told me if I kept taking the pain meds and drinking, I'd be dead sooner rather than later. That scared me— my life was a mess, but I didn't want to die—so I made some hard choices."

She was still silent, so he forced himself to look at her.

Her gaze was locked on him, reflecting what looked like a combination of sympathy, stunned shock and…something else he couldn't put his finger on. Something akin to regret, maybe? *That* didn't bode well.

"So you just…quit, cold turkey?" she asked.

"Pretty much. As soon as I got out of the hospital, I checked into a wonderful rehab center down there, went through detox—an experience I wouldn't wish on my worst enemy—met my counselor, Marv, and then the most extraordinary thing happened."

"What's that?"

"I found God."

She smiled crookedly, just the barest hint of one side of her mouth lifting. "He is truly amazing, isn't He?"

"He is," Curt replied. "He saved me."

Shaking her head, she said, "No, you saved yourself. God was just there to show you the way and help you when you faltered."

"I haven't faltered yet," he said. "Well, not since the overdose. I used to use pills to handle life. Now I depend on God."

"I can see that," she said. "You've made remarkable progress."

It was gratifying to know that others noticed the good in him. That day had been a long time coming. "Yes, I have."

She sat quietly for a second, looking down at her hands clenched in her lap. "You didn't steal those pain meds."

Something eased in his chest. "No, I didn't." He caught her gaze. "I can't tell you how much it means to me to hear you say that."

"I'm only telling the truth, and for the record,

I didn't believe you stole them when your dad accused you of it," she said.

"Thank you for your faith in me."

"What is it, exactly, that you're looking for now?" she asked.

He thought about her question. "Family. Stability. To eventually find someone who will love me, warts and all." He'd never really verbalized his wants and needs, but the past few weeks here in Moonlight Cove, with Jenna and Sam and everyone else, had hit home the truth. "I want happily ever after."

"I want that, too."

"But not with me," he said.

Her face twisted. "I told you. I let my heart rule my head with Garrett, and I can't make that mistake again. I'm sorry."

"You're just being honest, and that's as it should be."

"I sense a 'but' in there," she said.

He lifted a shoulder. "Sometimes honesty is brutal, and now I don't have the crutch of drugs anymore to help me deal. But I'll find a way. The fact that I'm even talking to you is a good sign."

"I hope you find what you're looking for."

I think I already have. He pressed his lips together; he didn't know what to say that hadn't already been said, so he just remained silent.

After a moment of quiet she retrieved her

crutches and started to get to her feet. "Well, it's late, and I'm beat."

He jumped up to help her.

She held out a hand. "No, I'm fine."

Yes. She was fine on her own. He understood that now. So he simply fell back and let her be.

She got herself situated with her crutches, and after hanging her head for a bit, she said, "I admire how you've overcome so many challenges."

He wanted to say he didn't want her admiration—he wanted her respect. Her love. To be the man who would make her dreams come blissfully true. But he didn't say any of that. Begging wasn't his style, and he was what he was, complicated past and all. No changing that. So instead he simply said, "Thank you."

She hobbled away, and when she reached the door, she turned. "I think you're going to be just fine."

He inclined his head in acknowledgment, staying silent. A response seemed useless.

She gave him one last baleful look, and then she turned, pushed the door open with one of her crutches and was gone.

The door clunked behind her.

Curt stayed for a long moment, his head bowed, her words echoing in his mind. Fine. Yeah, sure, he'd be fine. And clean, sober and a part of his family again, just as he wanted.

Why didn't that seem like enough?

* * *

Jenna closed the porch door behind her and sagged back against it, her eyes shut, her legs shaking so much she feared her crutches wouldn't hold her up. The hurt look that had bloomed on Curt's face when she'd told him he wasn't the man for her rose in her mind. Her throat thickened and her eyes burned.

Had she made a mistake? Was she being too cautious? Too picky?

"You look upset, dear."

Jenna's eyes popped open. Miss Landry stood in the far end of the foyer near the kitchen, dressed in a light blue terry-cloth robe and slippers. "Yes, I guess I am."

"I take it you and Mr. Graham had a difficult conversation?" Miss Landry said, a knowing light in her eyes.

Jenna pushed off the door and rebalanced herself on her crutches. "Why do you think that?"

"My room is just below yours, and even closer to the porch."

"Did we keep you awake?" Jenna asked, hobbling closer.

"Goodness, no. You know I sleep like a rock normally. Tonight, I woke up with a touch of heartburn, and when I got up to get my medicine, I heard you two out there."

Jenna's face warmed and she studied the floor.

"Don't worry, I didn't hear any details." Miss Landry shuffled near. "But it doesn't take a crystal ball to know what you were more than likely talking about."

"It doesn't?" Was Jenna's attraction to Curt that obvious to everyone else?

"No, dear, it doesn't. I've seen the way the two of you look at each other. There's a connection there, right?"

Jenna went over and lowered herself onto the couch. The need to confide in someone was strong. She'd go crazy if she didn't. "Yes, there is," she admitted softly as she set her crutches aside.

Miss Landry sat down next to her. "No surprise. You're both young, single and attractive. The perfect conditions for a romance."

"I'm not sure I want a romance."

"Why not?" Miss Landry's eyes sparkled. "Love's a wonderful thing."

It hadn't been for Jenna. "I let my heart take over once before, when I shouldn't have, and it turned out badly. The relationship imploded, and I vowed I'd be more careful the next time I fell in love."

"Yes, you told me about your list."

"That's why I have that list. My boyfriend cheated on me, and I ignored all the warning signs. I let my attraction take over, and I regret it."

"Everyone has failed relationships in their past. I've had a few broken hearts of my own."

"No one in my family has ever had a broken heart," Jenna said. "They all lived happily ever after with their first love."

"Really? That's very unusual."

Jenna nodded. "My family isn't like most families. They succeed at everything." Most especially at matters of the heart.

"Hmm." Miss Landry looked pensive. "Well, I believe you. But perfection might be a bit lofty of a goal for most people."

"My family exudes lofty," Jenna said, rolling her eyes.

"I sense a little frustration with that loftiness."

"It's hard to come from a family of perfect people."

"I would imagine so," Miss Landry replied thoughtfully. "But maybe they're not as perfect as you think."

"Oh, they are, trust me."

"Appearances can be deceiving, you know."

"Not in this case. My family is exactly what they seem." Impossibly impeccable.

"What is it about Curt that has you doubting things?"

"You were there tonight at the potluck. You heard it all."

"Yes, I did. Curt has clearly had issues, and

his family situation is—*was*—a mess. But people change all the time." Miss Landry adjusted the belt on her robe. "And Curt's problems seem to be in the past."

"True, I know that on one level. But on another, I'm just so scared to let myself fall for him," Jenna said in a trembling voice. "I'm scared to get hurt."

"Love is scary. But worth it, from what I've seen. I wish I'd taken more of a risk," Miss Landry said in an all-knowing yet gentle tone.

A risk. Yes, letting Curt into her heart would be risky. And Jenna didn't think she was ready to face the danger.

On the heels of that thought, something occurred to Jenna. She turned so she was facing Miss Landry. "So, if you don't mind my asking, if love is so wonderful, why didn't you ever marry?"

"I was wondering if you'd get around to asking me that." Miss Landry studied her hands for a moment. "I was just like you regarding love— I was deeply hurt by a young man early on, and that made me idealistic, always on the hunt for the perfect man."

Jenna listened raptly. This story sounded uncomfortably familiar.

"Looking back, I realize I focused on the negative rather than the positive, and no man could ever measure up." A sad light entered Miss Landry's eyes. "I was *too* picky, and before I knew it, I was past middle age and alone. By that time I was used to being alone, and that made it even harder to find someone who would fit in with my unrealistic picture of what I wanted."

Jenna's heart contracted painfully. "So you never did find the perfect love."

"Correct. And I regret it deeply now."

"You do?" Jenna asked in a hushed voice.

"Definitely. I'm not saying you should settle for just any man. But perhaps you should broaden your scope just a bit. It would be a shame for you to end up alone like I did."

Miss Landry's words raised all sorts of questions in Jenna's mind. Did she really want to end up by herself, filled with regret, wishing she'd taken a different path? Wishing she hadn't been so discerning?

She'd need to figure out the answers to those questions before it was too late and Curt moved on. Before he found someone else who could love him the way he deserved to be loved.

Living with eternal regret wasn't something she wanted to contemplate.

Chapter Fourteen

A week after the potluck, Jenna went to church with Curt. They'd been amicable, but not as close as they'd been before. Jenna had done her best to deal with feeling as if a piece of her heart had broken off. She was still so confused by her and Curt's "relationship," but she was frozen in indecision. Thankfully he hadn't pushed the matter, and Jenna had simply let herself float in limbo, neither committing nor cutting things off completely.

After the church service the following Sunday, she and Curt walked into the foyer. Thankfully she was able to walk without crutches now.

"Hi, Miss Jenna!" Sam said, catching up with them. The boy was wearing a pair of dark blue pants and a long-sleeved white button-up shirt. Guess his mom had taken pity on him and hadn't made him wear a tie. Either that, or he'd ditched the thing long ago.

"Hey, Sam," she said, putting her arm around him and giving him a squeeze. He and his mom had been sitting three pews in front of them, and Jenna had noticed his fidgeting barely a quarter of the way through the sermon.

Curt stuck out his hand. "How're you doing, Mr. Waters?" he asked with a wink.

Sam shook Curt's hand. "Good." He held up a piece of paper. "Look what I made in Sunday school."

Jenna looked at what he'd held up. "Oh, a collage. I used to love to make stuff like that."

"Yep, one of those," Sam said. "We were supposed to make a collage about all of the important people in our lives using pictures cut from magazines."

With keen interest, Curt bent down to study the piece. "Tell us about this."

"Okay." Sam pointed to a picture of what looked like a large hotel, then to photos of baking supplies and a heart. "This picture is about Miss Jenna 'cause she owns a hotel and bakes stuff and 'cause I like her."

Jenna pressed a hand to her chest, touched. "Oh, Sam, that's so sweet."

He moved his hand. "And this is a picture of an office and a cat and a car because my mom works in an office, loves our cat and has a cool car."

"That's great, Sam," Jenna said.

He shifted his fingers. "And this is a picture of some sports stuff and a guitar and a man because Mr. Graham works at a sports store, plays guitar and is nice."

Jenna looked at Curt. He seemed completely dumbfounded. "You put me in your collage?" he said, his voice sounding huskier than usual. Clearly he was deeply affected by Sam's including him in the collage. What could be more endearing?

"Well, yeah," Sam said. "You're one of my bestest friends." He slid his gaze to Jenna. "I mean, *best* friends."

Curt blinked several times and his mouth worked for a second. "Sam, I can't tell you how much that means to me."

Jenna swallowed, trying to dislodge the lump forming there. "Same goes for me," she said. "Thank you, Sam. This is lovely."

Sam's mom, Susan, walked up. She wore a cream-colored skirt and dark brown blouse that matched her eyes and had her blond hair pulled back into a bun. "Hi, Jenna, Curt." She'd met Curt a few days ago when she'd picked Sam up at the inn.

"Hello, Susan."

"Hi, Susan," Curt said.

"Sam was just showing us the collage he made in Sunday school."

Susan smiled. "It's great, isn't it? You two rate pretty high on his list."

"After you, they're my favorite people," Sam said.

"I know, sweetie." Susan turned her attention to Jenna. "Um, Jenna, could I talk to you for a minute?"

"Sure." Susan probably wanted to discuss the day-care schedule for the upcoming school holidays, or something like that.

"Alone?" Susan whispered, her mouth tight.

Alarm niggled at Jenna. Nodding, she looked at Curt. "Would you hang here with Sam for just a bit?"

"Of course." Curt looked at Sam. "Hey, bud. You wanna go outside and enjoy the sunshine?"

"Yeah!" Sam said.

"We'll just come out there when we're done," Jenna said.

"See you then." Curt and Sam headed out the front doors, which had been thrown open wide.

Jenna turned to Susan, trying to stay calm despite Susan's demeanor. "What's up?"

Susan's brow wrinkled. "I just had a call from the police."

"Oh, no." Jenna reached out and put a hand on Susan's arm. "Why?"

Susan let out a heavy breath. "Apparently my

ex-husband escaped from a prison work crew earlier this morning. He's currently at large."

Jenna's breath caught. "You're kidding."

"I wish I were." Susan chewed on her lip. "The police want to talk to me, and I'd rather not take Sam with me to the station. Would it be possible for you to take him for a while?"

"Of course. He can stay with me for as long as you need."

"Thank you," Susan said, her voice audibly shaky.

"Are you scared?"

"Yes, I am." Susan crossed her arms over her middle. "Sid went to jail for felony assault because he assaulted me and a man I dated after Sid and I divorced. He's dangerous, and I felt a lot safer knowing he couldn't get to me when he was locked up."

Jenna was horrified; she'd never known the details of why Sam's father was in jail. Clearly, Sam's dad was a violent man. "Well, I'll help in any way I can. Sam is welcome at my house anytime."

"Thank you. I really appreciate you being so kind to Sam, and Curt's kindness, too. You're both wonderful people, and you've both clearly had a big influence on him. I thank God every day for bringing you into our lives."

Jenna's heart squeezed. "That's so sweet of you

to say. I'm just happy I've had the chance to have Sam in my life, and I'm sure Curt feels the same way." She had a feeling Sam had a big effect on Curt; Curt's reaction to the collage was testament to that. She was glad; Curt needed as many positive relationships in his life as he could get.

That thought had her heart squeezing and her eyes burning. She wouldn't be one of those positive relationships. At least not in a romantic sense.

Clamping down on her emotions, willing her tears away, Jenna headed out the front door with Susan by her side, looking for the guys. The sun was shining at the moment, and puffy clouds dotted the September sky like cotton. A nice breeze, fresh with a salty tang, blew in from the ocean only a few blocks away.

Curt and Sam stood in the grass next to the walkway that led to the church.

Sam ran over, waving a blade of grass. "Mr. Graham is teaching me how to whistle with grass."

"That's cool," Susan said. "I was never very good at that."

Jenna looked at Curt. The sun glinted off his hair and he looked very handsome in his dark pants and light blue shirt, the exact color of the sky at his back. She tried not to stare too hard. "Very cool." He seemed to have a knack for finding interesting things to teach Sam, and Sam ate it all up. The two had clearly formed a bond.

"Honey, I have an errand to go run," Susan said to Sam. "You're going to go home with Miss Jenna for a while."

"I am?" Sam jumped up and down. "Yay!"

Susan hugged her son. "I'll be by later to pick you up."

"Okay. Bye, Mom."

"Thank you again, Jenna." Susan waved and hurried to her car in the nearby parking lot.

Curt ambled over. "Well, it looks like you're stuck with us, Sammy," he said in a clearly teasing tone. "I think this calls for ice cream."

"Ice cream? Really?" Sam exclaimed. "I never get ice cream during the day."

"It isn't even noon yet," Jenna put in. "We haven't even had lunch."

"Do we have to have a schedule for ice cream?" Curt asked, shoving his hands into his pockets.

"Um, well…" Jenna tapped her chin, thinking, trying to come up with a valid response. Actually, ice cream sounded good….

Sam tugged on her sleeve. "Please, can we go, Miss Jenna? It sounds so fun."

"Yes, it would be fun." Curt rubbed his belly. "And delicious."

Jenna looked from Sam's hopeful face to Curt's. She was outnumbered, and didn't stand a chance.

Besides, why be a stick-in-the-mud? Maybe a fun outing would lighten her spirits. "Okay, okay, ice cream it is."

Sam whooped. "Yes!"

"But when we get home, we have to work on school stuff," she said to Sam in a staid tone.

"My homework is at my house," Sam replied.

"I'll think of something else to do, then," Jenna said, hiking her purse up onto her shoulder. "I know how to make flash cards, you know."

"Okay, whatever you say," Sam said with a big grin. "Ice cream is worth it."

Jenna chuckled, then turned to Curt. "Should we walk?" I Scream for Ice Cream was only a few blocks from the church.

He held out his arm for her, his brown eyes glowing in the sunshine. "Yes, let's. It's a perfect day for it."

His smile did funny things to her insides, made her feel all fluttery and warm at the same time. She took his arm, trying not to let the feel of his firm biceps beneath her fingers rattle her too much.

But that, along with the memory of his touching reaction to Sam's collage fresh in her mind, she had a feeling that staying calm, cool and collected this afternoon was a pipe dream. And something that wouldn't be cooled off even if she applied her ice cream directly to her fore-head instead of eating it.

"Are you sure you can eat all that?" Jenna asked Sam.

As he tried to smile, Sam licked the giant ice-cream cone he'd just been handed as they stood in front of the counter of I Scream for Ice Cream, Phoebe Sellers's store on Main Street. "Yup, no problem."

"Where does he put it all?"

Curt shrugged. "He's a growing boy, right, Sam?"

"Right," Sam mumbled around a huge glob of ice cream.

Tanya, Phoebe's lone employee who'd taken over full-time for her while she and Carson were on their honeymoon, handed Curt his cone. It was, if possible, even bigger than Sam's.

Jenna eyed the dessert monstrosity sideways. "What's your excuse?" she asked with a crook of her brow.

Curt paused, his head cocked. He liked this teasing side of her. "Um…I don't have one." He licked his cone. "Except maybe that I love ice cream."

"No kidding," Jenna said.

"Here you go," Tanya said, holding up a cone

for Jenna that looked positively teensy compared to Sam's and Curt's.

"Aw, that's just pitiful," Curt said, looking at her cone with an exaggerated frown. "Don't you think so, Sam?"

"Yup. I like mine better." He grinned, exposing the space where he'd lost a tooth last night. "It's hum-on-gous," he said, drawing the word out.

Jenna eyed her cone. "This is what I always order."

"I'm sorry," Curt said with a lift of his brow.

"Yeah." Sam snortled. "Me, too."

She raised her chin. "Ice cream has a lot of fat and calories."

"So?" Curt said.

"So…I need to eat less of it."

"You can't tell me you need to worry about that," Curt replied, keeping his eyes on her face. "You're very slender."

She blinked. "Well…not exactly." She glanced at her cone. "This is just what I always get."

"So you said. Maybe you need to take a chance and order something outrageous." She worked so hard, juggled so many things. She deserved a treat.

"Yeah, Miss Jenna," Sam piped in, hopping up and down. "Order something really 'rageous."

Curt took a bite of his ice cream. "Yum, this is so good," he said, rolling his eyes. "You definitely deserve a super-duper cone." He grabbed a napkin from the stainless-steel napkin holder on the counter. "Go crazy."

She glanced at her piddly cone again. "All right, I'll get more." She gave her cone back to Tanya, who'd been standing by, quietly observing the interplay about the ice cream, clearly waiting for Jenna's decision. "Would you please add another scoop of chocolate chip and another of mocha almond fudge, please."

"A three scooper, coming right up," Tanya said.

"A three scooper." Curt fist-bumped Sam. "Yes! She's come over to our side."

"Woo-hoo, Miss Jenna," Sam crowed, his face wreathed in glee.

A stunning smile lit her face. "I figure I might as well give in to you two ice-cream fools." Tanya handed her revised cone back to her. "Though when I agreed to dessert, I didn't envision this kind of treat."

Sam held up his hand. "Yours is even giganter than mine."

"More gigantic," Jenna said without missing a beat. "And we need to eat faster and get some bowls in case we can't wolf these down before they melt."

"Coming right up." Tanya grabbed three plastic bowls and handed them to Jenna. "Drips are expected, though, so no worries."

A few moments later, Curt settled next to Jenna at one of the tables Phoebe had set up around the store.

"Don't get any ideas, mister," Jenna said immediately to Sam, who was eyeing the candy lining one wall of the store. "You already have enough sugar in front of you to last three days."

Sam nodded. "I know. I just love candy," he said wistfully.

"Me, too," Curt added. "What's your favorite?"

"Gummi Bears," Sam replied between bites of ice cream. "Or maybe Mike and Ikes."

"Mike and Ikes are good, sure." Curt pondered that for a moment. "But if I had to choose, I'd probably choose Hot Tamales."

"I've never had those. My mom says they're hot," Sam said.

Tanya arrived with some plastic spoons. "Thought you might need these if your cones get out of control."

Curt took the spoons and put them down in the middle of the table. "Thanks." He looked back at Sam. "Well, maybe, but Hot Tamales are good. My brothers and I used to see who could eat the most."

"Who won?" Sam asked, his eyes bright with curiosity.

"Well, I'd like to say I did, but I can't. My brother Seth was always the champion Hot Tamale eater." Curt plunked his ice-cream cone down in his bowl, cone up. "Wouldn't it be cool if someone made Hot Tamale ice cream?"

"Or maybe Gummi Bear ice cream. My dad loves Gummi Bears, so that's why I love them." Sam scrunched up his face. "He also likes those candy bars with the yucky coconut in them."

"Yeah, those are gross," Curt said.

"Speak for yourself," Jenna said tartly. "I happen to like coconut."

"Ugh," Curt said, shuddering.

"Yuck." Sam cringed.

Then they laughed, cohorts in teasing her. Boy, did it feel good to banter.

"Oh, I see what's happening here," Jenna commented with a teasing tone. "You guys are two peas in a pod."

"That's what my mom says about me and my dad."

Curt spoke up at the mention of Sam's dad. "You must miss him a lot."

"Yeah, I do." Sam's voice had a glum edge to it that made Curt ache.

"I bet." Curt picked up a spoon and swirled it in the puddle of quickly melting ice cream in his bowl. "You wanna talk about it?" he asked, echoing the words he'd heard Marv say a hundred times. And though the words were imitations, it still felt really good to offer a shoulder to Sam.

Sam shrugged. "I dunno." He fiddled with a spoon. "It makes me sad, so I just don't think about it all the time."

"I get that," Curt replied after a moment. He was—*had been*—a master at holding back.

Sam gazed up at Curt, his eyes wide. "You do?"

"Yeah." Curt put his spoon down and turned his full attention on Sam. "My dad wasn't around much when I was your age, and it made me sad, too." He was surprised how easy it was to talk about his past when Sam's well-being was at stake.

"Was he in jail, too?" Sam asked in a small voice.

Curt shook his head. "No, he wasn't. But he… had a lot of other distractions, and he wasn't around much."

"Did you miss him?" Sam asked.

Curt paused as all the trauma of his childhood came back full force. He cleared his throat. "Yes, I did."

Sam ate a spoonful of melted ice cream. "Is he around now?"

"He lives here in town," Curt said carefully. He didn't want to get into the nitty-gritty of his and his dad's relationship, most especially not with a kid. But it was important for Sam to know he wasn't alone in missing his dad.

"So you see him a lot?" Sam questioned.

"Um…" Curt tensed his mouth. "Not really." He didn't want to lie, but he had to tread lightly here.

"Why not, if he's here?" Sam shifted in his seat, then drew his legs up underneath himself. "If my dad was here, I'd want to be with him all the time."

Curt froze as the truth of Sam's statement hit home. Very deliberately he laid both forearms on the table, his eyes down, trying to figure out how to respond.

After a few long seconds, he just went with honesty. "You know, Sam, I hadn't thought about it that way."

"Well, maybe you should," Sam said, as if what he was suggesting was as obvious as the fact that the sky was blue. His childlike rationale impressed Curt. If this little kid could have such a positive attitude, couldn't Curt?

"Maybe I should," Curt said quietly.

"That's what I would do," Sam said. "If my dad was with me, I'd want to play with him all the time."

Affection for Sam warmed up Curt. He smooshed the boy's hair. "You've given me a lot to think about, Sam." And a lot to emulate.

"Miss Jenna helped me with that," Sam said, jamming another spoonful of ice-cream soup into his mouth.

Not surprising. Jenna was full of positive energy. "Oh, she did, did she?" Curt said to Sam, but he was looking at Jenna with his lips quirked.

"Yup. She's smart, and wants to be a teacher, so she knows how to teach stuff."

"She is pretty smart, isn't she?" Curt said truthfully, still holding her green gaze.

"Oh, stop, you two," she said with a wave of her hand. "I'll get a big head if you keep up with your flattery."

Sam squinted at her. "Why would your head grow from that?"

She chuckled. "It's an expression, honey. It means someone will think they're cooler than they are just because someone says nice things about them."

"But you are cool." Sam shoved his half-eaten ice cream away and leaned on the table in Curt's direction. "Don't you think she's cool, too?"

"I sure do, Sam." He hit her with a direct stare. "She's one of the coolest people I know. And the nicest, too. I wish I'd had someone like Miss Jenna in my life when I was your age." If he had, he was pretty sure his life would have turned out differently.

She stared back, her green eyes holding on his. Something elemental passed between them, and for a second, neither one spoke. Then Jenna flushed and pulled her gaze away. "Oh, that's so sweet," she said. "But I think you're exaggerating."

"No, I'm not. You're a wonderful influence, Jenna. Sam is lucky to have you in his life."

Curt only wished he could be so lucky now.

Chapter Fifteen

"Why didn't you want a guitar lesson, Miss Jenna?"

Jenna, Sam and Curt had returned home after ice cream, and now Jenna and Sam were doing the promised schoolwork after Curt had given Sam an impromptu guitar lesson. The truth pressed against her lips. *Because I have to keep my distance from the fascinating guitar teacher.*

Not that Jenna could say that to Sam. But she'd repeat it to herself as much as she had to in order to protect herself. Hearing Curt and Sam discuss their fathers at the ice-cream parlor and watching how patient and creative Curt was with Sam during their guitar lesson had just about melted every cell in her body.

But all of that wasn't for public consumption, especially not for an interested but had-to-remain-in-the-dark seven-year-old.

So she told another version of the truth. "I told you, sweetie." She held up some homemade flash cards she'd whipped up a few minutes ago during Sam's guitar lesson. "I want to help you with your spelling."

"Can't Mr. Graham help me?" Sam whined. "He sings stuff and plays the guitar."

"I think Mr. Graham has other things to do."

"Yeah, he left fast to go upstairs," Sam said with a frown.

Curt had hightailed it to his room after they'd each tripped over themselves trying to get out of an up-close-and-personal guitar lesson.

"I wonder why," Sam said.

Because Curt was clearly trying to avoid her as much as she was trying to avoid him. Her heart clutched a little, and she wavered in her resolve to keep Curt at a distance. He wasn't the man for her right now. It was too much too fast. She had to be cautious. This was just the way it had to be.

"I think he's just really busy, what with his job and everything," she said to avoid revealing too much.

Sam harrumphed. "Maybe you two can help me with my spelling together."

"We're doing just fine without him, don't you think?" she said, putting on a bright smile she didn't feel. "We only have a few more cards to go."

"He's more fun." Sam pouted. "Plus, we're both boys."

Poor Sam. He obviously needed a male influence in his life. Maybe she'd talk to Curt about spending more quality time with Sam. Sam loved him, and they did have fun together. And Curt was so wonderful with Sam, so gentle and kind—

She stopped short. A chill went through her as she realized in her unedited musings that Curt *was* a good role model for Sam. Someone she'd want Sam to spend time with. A fine man with nothing but good intentions. But he wasn't the kind of man that fit in with her future.

She wrinkled her brow, turning over her inequitable thoughts. Was her thinking about Curt being the wrong man for her flawed? Was Miss Landry right? Was she being too hasty? Too idealistic?

And…why was she operating on such a double standard? She'd missed him so much in the past week. Did that mean something profound? Something she wouldn't get over as she'd told herself she would when she'd found herself wanting to seek him out just to talk? Or listen to him play guitar and sing, his beautiful voice strumming her heartstrings?

A myriad of questions crowded her brain, overwhelming her. But she felt her foundation quake and begin, ever so slightly, to crumble at its base.

Another chill skated through her. Had she

made a big mistake in keeping Curt away from her heart?

A knock on the door cut off her chaotic musings. "Oh, that must be your mom," she said, looking at her watch. Jenna got to her feet to answer the door, again thankful her ankle was healed enough for her to walk without the crutches.

Sam flopped back on the couch, his arms crossed over his chest, still sulking. "I don't want to go home until Mr. Graham helps me with my spelling."

Jenna headed to the door, limping slightly. "Didn't he say he'd give you another lesson tomorrow if you studied your spelling with me tonight?"

"Yes," Sam groused.

"Well, then, let's keep on that track." She unlocked the door and opened it, expecting to see Sam's mom.

But a strange man stood there—holding a wicked-looking knife in his right hand.

With her heart in her throat, Jenna went to slam the door.

His hand shot out just fast enough to keep the door from closing. "Not so fast." He kicked the door with a booted foot, flinging it open so hard it crashed against the entry wall. "I'm coming in."

With hot panic rising in a choking tide, Jenna

stumbled back, her ankle letting out a painful twinge. Instinctively, she screamed, high and shrill.

The stranger lunged and grabbed her by the shoulders, cutting off her scream. "Quiet!" he demanded hoarsely, jamming a sticky hand across her mouth. His foul-smelling breath washed over her in a sickening wave. He spun her around and put her in a headlock, one hand still slanted over her mouth, the other hand holding the knife against her neck.

Breathing heavily, she struggled against his grip, trying to work herself free. She had to protect Sam and Miss Landry!

"Hold still," her assailant grunted in her ear. "I'm not gonna hurt you if you cooperate."

"Daddy?"

The man froze and his head swung left, the hand over Jenna's mouth going slack. "Sammy! There's my boy."

Understanding crashed down around Jenna. This man was Sam's dad, Sid Waters.

An escaped felon. He'd come here. To get Sam?

"Daddy," Sam said, coming into Jenna's line of vision. "Why do you have that knife on Miss Jenna's throat?"

The knife eased a bit.

"I've come to get you, son, and I had a feeling Miss Jenna here might pose a problem."

Jenna's gut clenched nauseatingly. He was

going to kidnap Sam! She thrashed about, trying to escape.

Sid jerked her close, his headlock clamping tighter. "Hold still, lady, or you'll be sorry." The knife bit against her neck.

Jenna's heart beat so hard it felt as if it was going to burst from her chest. She nodded, buying time. Maybe she could disarm him somehow....

"I thought you were in jail," Sam said, frowning.

"I was," Sid replied. "But I got myself assigned to a work crew along the highway, and me and my buddy Cobra escaped." Sid snorted derisively. "Piece of cake, pulling one over on those stupid guards. I remembered Miss Jenna's name, and after a computer search, thanks to Cobra's brother's laptop, I came straight here to get you, Sammy-boy. He's waiting outside in his brother's car. We got ourselves a plan to go to a place Cobra knows." Sid chortled in glee. "No one'll find us there, and you and me can finally be together, Sam."

Stark panic and rolling dread engulfed Jenna in a breath-stealing tide. She couldn't let this lunatic take Sam. Sam's father or not, he was clearly an irrational criminal bent on kidnapping his own son, for goodness' sake.

A prayer wound through her brain. *Lord, pro-*

tect Sam from this crazy man, and give me the strength to be brave enough to foil his insane plan.

"You aren't going to hurt Miss Jenna, are you?" Sam asked, backing up toward the staircase to the rear of the room, his eyes wide. "She's nice."

Sid dragged her to the couch. "She'll be fine if she does what I say." He flung her down on the sofa, brandishing the knife. Then he pulled a roll of duct tape from the pocket of his oversize sweatshirt. "I'm going to tie you up, Miss Jenna, real quick, so no funny business."

"Don't do this," she implored in a harsh whisper, flinging her hair out of her face. "Think about Sam."

"I've done nothing but think about Sam for two years," Sid snarled, his attention solely on her. "And now I want my boy." He yanked off a piece of tape. "Hold out your arms."

Just then she spied Curt peek his head out from around the corner that led to the staircase behind Sid. Curt! Yes! He was here. He must have heard her scream. Hope blossomed, and doubled when Sam caught sight of Curt, too, and ran into his outstretched arms. Smart boy.

Curt pressed a hand to his lips and then made a rolling sign, signaling her to play along. Then he turned and put Sam down behind himself, out of sight. Sam was safe.

She instantly held out her hands, her arms quivering.

With one hand, Sid roughly wrapped the tape around her wrists, binding them together. "Now your feet."

She lifted her feet.

Just as Sid bent to bind her feet with the tape, Curt launched himself at him like a mountain lion, kicking the knife from the man's hand.

Sid spun around with a roar.

Curt rushed Sid, but Sid got the jump on him and landed a punch to Curt's forehead just above his right eye. Curt let out a grunt.

Sid sniggered. "Gotcha, hero-man."

Wincing, Jenna grabbed for the cordless phone. But it wasn't on the base. She darted her gaze around. Where was it? Her eyes went back to the battle.

Curt stayed upright somehow, and with nary a hesitation, despite the blow he'd taken, let out a bellow. Jenna watched as he attacked, striking Sid with a wicked fast, hard-hitting right cross to his bald head.

Sid went down like a brick wall, landing on the floor in a heap. Panting, Curt danced back, his dukes still up, watching Sid for a few seconds to be sure he was down. Then, with a victorious flourish, he planted his foot on Sid's back.

He swung around, his jaw tense, his frantic gaze searching for Jenna and Sam.

He sagged when he saw them. He met Jenna's gaze, his dark eyes holding on hers. "You guys all right?"

Her throat clogged, and all she could do was nod.

"Good."

Miss Landry, dressed in a blue robe and white hairnet, stepped into the room from the hallway, the cordless phone held high. "I called 911," she said with a satisfied smile. "The police are on their way."

Quaking, Jenna hooked her taped hands over Sam's head and hugged him close, tears forming in her eyes, relief pouring through her in a welcome tide. They were safe. All of them. Because of Curt.

Thank You, God, for answering my prayers. And for Curt, who saved us with his bravery and quick thinking.

Something melted inside of her, freeing a frozen part of her heart.

The police arrived, took Curt's, Jenna's and Miss Landry's statements, and then carted a conscious Sid Waters off in handcuffs. A frantic Susan Waters arrived shortly after the police, scooping Sam up in her arms and holding him close. After a talk with the police, she left with Sam, who was holding up amazingly well. Curt figured maybe Sam didn't understand exactly what had transpired. Either way, with his mom and Jenna taking care of him, Curt was sure Sam would be fine.

Curt had refused any kind of medical care. A black eye was a black eye and he'd deal. He'd suffered much worse physically over the years. He could handle a bruised face.

Shortly after the house was quiet, he went in search of Jenna, needing to make sure she was okay. He found her standing by the counter in the kitchen, a cup of tea in front of her, staring off into space. Just the sight of her made his breath catch.

"How're you doing?" he asked quietly, moving into the room.

She turned, her face ghostly pale. "I'm still shaking," she said, holding out a trembling hand.

He took her small hand in his own. "Me, too. That was a scary situation."

"Yes, it was," she said, her voice breaking. Her lips quivered, and then her face crumbled. "I was so frightened." Tears welled and fell. "If he had taken Sam, I don't know what I would have done."

Curt didn't know what he would have done, either. Just the thought of Sam or Jenna being hurt, or taken, had Curt's pulse racing in dread once more.

Seeing them in danger had absolutely petrified him. A bone-deep terror that had frozen his insides and let loose every protective instinct he possessed. Going after Sid Waters hadn't been a choice. It was something organic that had materialized the second he'd seen Jenna with a knife against her throat.

Going with his instincts, he put his arms around Jenna and pulled her close. He pressed his face into her soft hair, inhaling the smell of her lemony shampoo. "But he didn't take him, so everything is fine."

She leaned into him, snaking her arms around his waist, holding tight. "Thanks to you."

"I just did what anyone would," he whispered. "No biggie."

"It is a biggie," she replied, her breath warm against his chest. "You went after a man with a knife without hesitation." She pulled back and looked at him with watery eyes. "You could have been seriously hurt." She suppressed a sob and pressed herself against him again, tighter this time. "Another thing I don't want to think about."

Her concern made his chest collapse. "But I wasn't badly hurt, and Sam and you are safe."

After a long moment, she pulled back and looked at him, her brow creased. "You're going to have a nasty shiner." She lifted her hand to his face but didn't touch him. "It looks like it hurts."

"It does," he said, roaming his gaze over her face. "But I'll live." Being close to her was the best medicine in the world.

She nodded. "Thank You, God."

"Yes, thank You, Lord," he said, looking up. "You watched over all of us today, and we're grateful."

He sought her gaze and her liquid green eyes stared back. Drawn to her, he honed in on her rosy lips, slowly bending down—

"Is everybody okay in here?" Miss Landry said from the door to the kitchen, sending a jolt of alarm through Curt.

He jumped back and so did Jenna. A becoming flush of color built in her cheeks.

"We're fine, Miss Landry," Jenna said in an unnaturally high voice, smoothing her hair back with one hand. "Um, can I interest you in some tea? The water's already hot."

Miss Landry came into the kitchen. "That sounds wonderful, my dear." She looked at Curt's face. "You need some frozen peas on that."

"Yes, you do." Jenna shook her head and rolled her eyes. "How could I have forgotten that?"

"You've had your mind on other things," Miss Landry said. "We all had a big scare tonight."

"I've got some peas in the freezer in the garage," Jenna said. "Let me get them."

"I'm fine," he said. "You don't need to take care

of me." Though the fact she wanted to made him feel good. Cared for.

It was a heady feeling he could get used to fast. But he wouldn't.

Jenna swung around. "Yes, I do. You took care of Sam and me, so I need to take care of you. Simple as that." She pointed to one of the chairs by the kitchen table. "Sit down while I get you some frozen peas." She left the room.

He looked at Miss Landry, quirking his mouth up at one corner. "She's bossy."

"Yes, she is, when necessary," she said, her blue eyes sparkling. "She wants to take care of you."

He sat down. "I guess I'm not used to that."

"Must feel nice, then," Miss Landry said, joining him at the table.

"Actually, it does," he said truthfully. "She's a good person."

"Yes, she is, and women like her are hard to come by." Miss Landry gave him a direct stare. "You shouldn't let her slip away."

His heart blipped, but Jenna's arrival with his makeshift ice pack precluded any kind of response, if he'd had one. As it was, he was speechless.

"Okay, here we go," Jenna said. "Peas for you."

Miss Landry shot him another significant look, and then settled back in her chair.

Curt took the bag and pressed them against his face.

"Miss Landry, let me get you your tea," Jenna said, bustling over to the cupboard and getting a mug out.

Curt watched her in action with his free eye, struck once again by her attitude. Here she'd been involved in fending off a man with a knife and a near abduction, and she was taking care of him and Miss Landry.

His stomach dropped. Miss Landry was right. Jenna was a rare find, a woman to hold on to with both hands. But how could he hold on to her if she wouldn't let him?

Curt arrived at work early the morning after the abduction incident, weary from lack of sleep, thanks to his bruised face. Since any kind of medication was out of the question, he had just endured the pain throughout the night. Not fun, but necessary.

To his surprise, his dad was waiting for him by the front door of the store.

Great. This oughta be good, having his dad come and knock him down first thing in the morning after the night he'd had. Yeah. Fun times.

"Dad." He unlocked the door and opened it, trying to ignore the ache in his face. "What are you doing here?"

His father followed him into the store. "I heard about what happened last night at the inn."

Curt raised his eyebrows, then winced. Man, that hurt. "News travels fast around here."

His father grunted. "Small town. Miss Landry called your mom, and she called me." He came closer and peered at Curt. "That's a nasty shiner."

"Yeah, but the other guy looks worse."

"I heard you knocked him out cold." Was that… pride in his dad's voice?

Curt had to be hearing wrong. He'd never done anything to make his father proud. "He had a knife to Jenna's throat and was bent on taking Sam." He jerked his neck sideways and heard it crack.

"I probably would have killed the jerk," his dad said, scowling. "A man has to protect what's his."

Jenna wasn't Curt's. Suddenly his heart ached as much as his face. "Right."

"You did a good thing last night."

"I was in the right place at the right time," Curt said as he headed over to the front counter. He couldn't get too excited about his father's praise. A knockdown would surely follow.

"No, it was more than that," Dad said. "I've seen a change in you lately. You came back to Moonlight Cove. You're doing a good job with the store. You're helping people."

Curt wanted to let Dad's praise in. But a lifetime of receiving the opposite made Curt wary. "Where is all of this approval coming from?"

His father grimaced. "I deserved that."

Curt just looked at him.

"I realize I haven't been a good father." He let out a big, shaky sigh. "I…never had a good role model for that."

"I know you had a rough childhood." Orphaned at ten. Living on a farm with neighbors who abused him. Being on his own at fifteen.

"Yeah, I did. And I've always had this anger roiling around inside of me because of that."

"Understandable," Curt said.

"Maybe. But lately I've come to see that I was way too hard on you boys."

"Yeah, coming over and accusing me of stealing your pain meds would qualify as 'hard,'" Curt said bitterly.

"Yeah, about that." Dad laid his hands on the counter. "My cleaning lady fessed up to stealing them."

Ah, the truth at last. "Well, I'm glad you figured it out."

"I fired her."

"Not surprising," Curt replied drily.

"I never should have accused you. You're clearly on a new path, one that doesn't involve drugs." He swallowed. "I'm sorry, son. Can you forgive me?"

Curt couldn't have been more surprised. "You're apologizing?" This was a first.

"Yes, yes, I am," Dad said, his voice gravelly. "You saved Jenna and Sam last night, you helped Jenna with that tea thing and Seth tells me you've done a wonderful job with the store."

Curt could only stare.

His father went on, "I'm proud of you, proud of the progress you've made. I didn't give you enough credit."

A chunk of rock formed in Curt's chest, but something else inside dissolved just a bit. His dad saw the good in him. Curt saw it in himself. Finally. "I've waited a long time to hear those words."

"Too long," his father said. "I'm a slow learner."

"Why are you learning at all?" Curt asked, curious about what had precipitated the change of heart. Dad wasn't exactly known for being open to new things. Or for letting emotions or relationships matter.

Dad grimaced. "Not like me, is it?"

Curt shook his head slowly.

"I've always been a tough guy, and that's really all I know."

"You had to be tough to survive your childhood," Curt said.

"Yes, I did." Dad drew in a shaky breath. "I

was determined to stay a tough guy, and I made a ton of mistakes because of it."

That resonated with Curt. He'd made lots of mistakes, too.

Dad went on, "I tried to soldier on after your mom left me, to be that tough guy, thinking that as long as I stayed strong, I'd be fine."

"How's that working for you?" Curt asked, repeating Marv's oft spoken words.

"Not very well," Dad said in a husky voice. "You're back in town and we've never been further apart. Seth doesn't want me around the kids, and your mom…well, she won't have anything to do with me." He blinked several times. "I'm losing my family."

"Yes, you are," Curt replied. No sense in not being honest.

Dad swiped a hand over his eyes. "I've come to realize that I lost something precious when your mom and I split up, and I'll never get it back. And I have no one to blame but myself."

Curt agreed, but he stayed silent, letting Dad get it out.

"The divorce changed me, slowly, yes, but the change happened."

"So you regret the divorce?"

"Every day." He regarded Curt with sadness in his eyes. "I didn't realize what I had until it was gone. But I see now that unless I change, I'll lose the rest of you, and I don't want that."

"So you learned your lesson too late to save your marriage."

"Yeah, I did," Dad said in a voice tinged with obvious regret. "But at least one good thing came of the divorce."

"What's that?" Curt asked, hardly able to believe he and his father were having a civilized conversation.

"It made me realize that I'd better start changing my ways, or I'll lose more than your mom."

"*Do* you want us in your life?" Curt asked, his throat tight, elusive optimism mounting little by little, though a part of him was still guarded.

Dad ran a hand through his already messed-up hair. "Yes, I do. I'm getting older, and if I don't mend my fences now, I'm going to die a lonely man."

Curt shook his head, and it felt as if a little man was pounding an ice pick in his brain. "I'm surprised by this new attitude of yours."

His father inclined his head left. "Me, too. But there you have it." He looked right at Curt, his eyes alight with hope. "Do you think it's too late?"

Curt cleared his throat. "My counselor told me that mistakes simply help us learn what not to do."

His dad nodded.

Curt kept talking. "And a little boy told me

that if my dad was around I should be with him all the time."

The older man's mouth trembled. "Sometimes little kids are pretty smart."

Curt let out a trembling breath. "I've made my share of bad moves, hurt a lot of people, and I'm hoping for absolution. How can I deny you the very thing I want?" He held out a shaky hand.

His dad laid his callused hand in Curt's grip. "Are you sure? I've let you down your whole life."

"If I can evolve, so can you, so I'm sure. It's never too late for second chances."

His father's fleshy shoulders sagged. "I can't tell you how much this means to me."

"It means a lot to me, too," Curt told him, trying to keep his voice even. "I'd like to have a family to go with my new life."

"The family you've never had," Dad said, his voice cracking.

"You've never really had one, either." Curt came around the counter and looked at his dad, seeing the paunch, the gray hair, the lines and stubbly face. The flawed, aging man who'd found it within himself to ask for forgiveness. "Looks like we both win."

And then he hugged his dad for the first time in…well…forever.

And his dad hugged him back, his arms shaking.

Curt stood there in his father's embrace, feeling

reborn, a metaphor for the new life he'd found in God. Curt had moved beyond his past in the eyes of his father and it felt good. Right. Hope for his own future burst within.

Dad pulled away, wiping his eyes. "I do have one piece of advice for you, though."

"Shoot."

"Don't make the same mistake I did and let someone you love walk away."

Curt stiffened. "Who are you talking about?"

"Jenna. You're in love with her, aren't you?"

"Why do you say that?"

"Your mom told me."

"How does she know?"

"I dunno. She just said it was obvious."

Curt digested that.

"So," his father said pointedly before Curt could talk. "*Are* you in love with her?"

Curt sighed. "I don't know."

"What do you mean, you don't know?" his dad huffed. "It's not that hard. Do you want to be around her all the time?"

"Yeah."

"Do you find yourself thinking about her often?"

"Yup."

"How did you feel when you saw her in danger last night?"

Curt's neck tightened. "I was terrified I was going to lose her," he replied.

"You say terrified?"

"That's what I said."

"Then I say you're in love with the little lady. All the signs are there."

Something exploded in Curt's chest, and the truth was suddenly there, right in front of him. "You're right. I am in love with Jenna." Deeply. He loved everything about her. The sort of person she was. Her deep faith. Her kind, generous heart. All of it.

He loved Jenna Flaherty. But...he wasn't the man she wanted. He shook his head, causing an ache that didn't begin to match the pain in his heart. "She has a list, and I don't fit the bill."

"A list?" Dad snorted. "That's a bunch of hoo-ha all wrapped up in one big fat excuse."

"Excuse?"

"Yeah, excuse. You know, to protect herself? I know all about excuses 'cause I had a boatful to keep my life within the lines I thought I needed."

"It makes sense, but I'm still leery of confessing my feelings."

Dad leaned in. "Remember how you just said you were terrified to lose Jenna when you saw her in danger last night?"

Curt nodded.

"Well, I know from cold hard experience that

you will lose her for sure if you don't tell her how you feel, if you don't fight for her." He drilled him with a hard stare. "How's that for terrifying?"

A chill washed over Curt. "I...hadn't thought about it that way."

"Well, you should before it's too late. And people change their minds all the time, realize what's important." He smiled, one of the first genuine smiles Curt had seen in a long time. "Look at me. And you. We're new men."

Curt fell back a step, trying to take it all in. Everything he had said made perfect sense in his head. However, Curt's heart was still scared.

But...his father had made a one-eighty. Could Jenna do the same? Could she see the man Curt had become? Good question. One he'd have to ask her. As soon as he could.

And then he'd know once and for all if he had any kind of chance to have her in his life. If she could return his love.

Sharp-toothed anxiety chomped holes in his paper-thin confidence. Guess it was a good thing he had his family behind him now; if Jenna rejected him again, he was going to need his mom, dad and brothers more than ever in the days and weeks to come.

Chapter Sixteen

Hoping that baking would calm her nerves after the traumatic events of the night before, Jenna went to work in the kitchen. She had a recipe for chocolate-chip salted caramel bars she'd wanted to try for a while, so she got busy gathering the ingredients, hoping that puttering in the kitchen would distract her from her thoughts.

She got the dough together quickly, and as her stand mixer worked on blending the ingredients, she set about unwrapping the caramels, focusing on the repetitive nature of the task as a way to keep her mind occupied. Then she dumped the candy into the double boiler on the stove.

Nagging thoughts crept in as she added cream. It was bad enough she had to deal with a man forcing his way into her house and trying to abduct Sam. She also had to handle the new picture of Curt that had emerged in her mind last night. He'd protected all of them, acting without a thought for his own safety. He was quite a guy, no question. Brave. Loving. Funny. Good with Sam. Good singer. Hey. That was important.

He had an imperfect past, but he'd proven he was a fine man—

"I thought I might find you here."

She whirled and pressed a hand to her chest. Curt stood there.

"You scared me," she said, flipping the mixer off. She turned toward him, noting that the bruise on his face had actually gotten worse since last night.

"Sorry," he said, moving closer. "I guess you couldn't hear me come in above the sound of the mixer."

"Guess not." She frowned. "Plus, I'm a little jumpy since last night. What are you doing here in the middle of the day?" Curt usually didn't come home until later, after he closed the store. "Are you feeling okay? That's a pretty good black eye you've got going there."

"My dad offered to look after the store, so I decided to come home for a bit, maybe lie down for a while." He pointed to his shiner. "Hopefully get this headache to go away."

"Your *dad?*" As far as she knew, Curt and his dad weren't on speaking terms, especially since he'd accused Curt of stealing his pain meds. "What happened?"

"Believe it or not, he came by this morning and we had a talk."

"Oh, how did that go?" she asked, hoping for Curt's sake that his dad hadn't put him down as usual.

"Actually, it went great."

She blinked.

"He asked for my forgiveness for everything that's happened, and I gave it."

A warm spot throbbed beneath her breastbone. "That's good news," she replied, stirring the caramel. "Do you mind if I ask what brought that on?"

"Don't mind at all." Curt leaned a hip against the counter opposite Jenna. "He said he's learned a lot since he and Mom split, and that he doesn't want to go through the rest of his life alone, especially since he has grandkids now."

She nodded. "Sounds like he's given it a lot of thought."

"He also told me his cleaning lady admitted to stealing the pain meds."

"Hey, that's great." She shook her head. "I mean…it's not great she stole them, just great that he now knows for sure that you didn't take them."

"Knows *for sure?*" Curt asked, his dark gaze intent. "Was there doubt?"

"Not on my part," she said quickly, regretting her choice of words. "I told you that a week ago."

"Yes, you did. But telling someone something and actually believing what you say are two different things. Talk is cheap," he said.

Okay. Looked as if he had something to say. She reached out and turned off the burner under the caramel. "What's going on, Curt?" She put the spoon down and steeled herself for whatever he was going to send her way.

"It's just that now that my dad has seen the man I am isn't the same man I was in the past, I wonder if you can do the same."

Unease slid up her spine. "Why do you ask?"

"Honestly?"

"Just tell me what's on your mind."

He held up his hands. "Okay, I'll quit beating around the bush. Seeing you in danger last night, well, it made me realize that…I'm in love with you, Jenna. And I'm wondering if you can love me back as the man I am today, without the shadows of my past interfering."

All at once, a multitude of emotions skated through her. Joy. Surprise.

Stark fear.

Fear won out; she was petrified of letting Curt into her heart. Garrett had shown her that love was risky, even more so with a man who had such a complicated past. "I…don't know." Lame. But it was the best she had on the fly.

He stiffened. "That pretty much answers my question."

"I said I didn't know, not *no*," she said. "Don't I get a chance to think about it?"

"If you loved me, you wouldn't have to think about it." His eyes hardened. "You'd just know."

"Says who?" she retorted.

Her reply set him back a step. "That's just my opinion," he replied, his chin rising. "But the fact that you're hesitating…well, that tells me everything I need to know."

Her defenses rose. "So just because you've had an epiphany, I have to have one in the blink of an eye?"

"No, that's not what I meant," he said.

"But that's what you said," she said. She went on before he could reply, "You know what? I think you're scared, and not giving me a chance to process or search my heart is your way of dealing with that." She was frightened, too, so it was easy to see the reaction in him.

Was he running away? Was she?

"Maybe so—love is scary," he said. "But your hesitation speaks volumes."

"You're right," she said. "I feel the way I feel, and I'm not ready to say I love you." True enough. But was she letting fear hold her back from admitting her true feelings? Confusion spread through her. She was bungling this, badly.

His face went blank, but the kind of manufactured blank that meant the exact opposite, as if he was covering up his reaction. "That's what I thought."

She merely dipped her head in acknowledgment, not trusting herself to speak. She had to be careful, protect her heart at all costs.

"So, that settles that," he said, his voice carefully modulated, like a Curt robot set on Calm. "I guess I should tell you now that as soon as I can find a place to stay, I'm moving out."

Her stomach fell. He was leaving. "I guess that makes sense," she managed to say, controlling the panic eating away at her. She didn't want him to leave—

"Yes, it does, given the situation."

The situation. As in he loved her, and she... she needed more time. He wasn't willing to be patient. "Agreed."

He paused, his lips rolled in. "Well, I'm going to go back to work." He turned to leave.

"Curt, wait," she called, her hand held out.

He swung back, regarding her with a direct but highly impersonal gaze. He remained silent.

Conflict warred within her. She was confused. Unsure. And there was too much at stake for her to make a hasty decision. "I'm sorry," she said, dropping her hand. "I wish I could give you a different answer at this moment."

A sad light entered his eyes. "But you can't, and I have to respect that, even though I don't like it." With that, he spun around and walked out of the kitchen.

And Jenna was left standing there by herself, feeling as if she'd just lost her best friend. And as if she'd just made a big mistake.

One that was unfixable, permanent, and had the power to break her heart in the end.

Curt didn't come home at his usual time after work.

Once dinner was over and Jenna had cleaned up, Miss Landry left to go visit her sister. Edgy and sad, Jenna didn't have the heart to do any chores. So she hung around downstairs, trying to read a romance novel she'd had on her to-be-read list, hoping to see Curt when he returned, maybe talk some more. Feel her way around what was going on. Hash it out somehow.

Ease the ache in her soul.

But it was fruitless. The front door didn't open. No Curt. No talk. No peace for her.

Just about the time she'd reread the same page three times, the phone rang. Hope rose. Was Curt calling? She jumped to her feet and went to get it.

With shaking hands she picked up the cordless and clicked Talk. "Hello?"

"Hi, honey, it's Mom."

"Oh, hi, Mom," she said, her shoulders tensing. "Is something wrong?"

"Why do you ask that?"

"Because you usually only call on Sundays." Her mom was nothing if not predictable.

"I know. But I wanted to let you know I worked out the bill with Oakhurst and paid it online this morning."

"Oh, good," Jenna said, trying to infuse some enthusiasm into her voice.

"You sound down. Is everything all right?"

Guess her attempt to sound upbeat had failed. Jenna felt tears well, and she wished her mom hadn't called right now. Jenna always felt less sure of herself after their calls, and after what had happened with Curt earlier today, she wasn't certain she had the strength to have a conversation with her mom. "Um…I'm fine." She started walking as she talked, restless, needing to move.

"You don't sound fine," Mom said.

"I'm okay," Jenna replied in an even tone. "What's going on there tonight?" Maybe a subject change would head off any kind of deep discussion that might cause Jenna to fall apart.

"Not much." Her mother paused. "Your dad

is at a meeting, and I'm just rattling around the house alone."

Jenna headed into the living room, noting how vacant the room seemed. Maybe being alone was getting to her.

Her eyes burned.

"I thought you had your book club meeting on Monday nights." Mom was an avid reader, and had belonged to the same club for years. The group only read depressing literary fiction, and had stiff rules about how fast each member had to read. If you couldn't keep up with the schedule, you were out. She was pretty sure they had tests to verify things.

"Oh, I do," she said. "But I didn't get my pages in this month, so I'm not going."

"Really? You were the one who set the schedule to begin with." Mom was a notoriously fast reader, and usually had another book going on the side.

"I know," she said in a weak voice that Jenna rarely heard. "I've…had a lot of other things on my mind."

Frowning, Jenna turned and wandered back into the kitchen. It, too, was dark, empty and chilly. She cleared the lump forming in her throat. "You seem…off tonight." Jenna made an about-face and wandered back down the hall.

A sigh echoed through the phone line. "I guess I am."

"Why?" Mom never had off times. She was a pillar of control and master of flawless organization, as well as a bundle of endless energy. She worked killer hours, was healthy and fit, and maintained a perfect marriage on top of all that. She was, and always had been, a one-woman ball of perfection. Jenna wondered how she did it all without cracking.

Silence reverberated into the phone. Finally, her mom said, "Your dad and I are having some problems."

Jenna almost dropped the phone. *"You're kidding."*

"I am not. We had a fight earlier about something silly, and he stormed out of the house."

A gasp popped out of Jenna's mouth. "You and Dad had a fight?" She went back into the living room, trying to ignore its emptiness, and plopped down on the couch. "And Dad left mad?"

"Yes. Why is that so hard to believe?"

Jenna switched the phone to her other ear. "Um, because you and Dad never fight."

"We do, too. All couples have disagreements."

"No, Mom, not you and Dad. I've never seen you guys disagree." They were calm, controlled and loving at all times. Almost superhuman, actually.

"Well, we do." A hesitation. "Though we probably hid some of our trials from you and your brother when you were growing up to protect you."

"Probably?" Jenna scoffed. "Definitely. To me, you seemed like the perfect couple."

"We have a good marriage, don't get me wrong. But that's because we work at it constantly."

"You do?" Jenna said, pulling in her chin.

"Of course. Your dad and I both have our faults and quirks. We've actually been to counseling several times over the years to work things out, and have an appointment next week to help us get through this rough patch."

Jenna shook her head. "I feel like I'm hearing about some other family."

"I've hidden too much from you, I guess."

"It seems you have. But in a way, I'm relieved, actually."

"Why?"

"Because I've always felt so much pressure to have a perfect love like you and Dad do."

"Oh, honey, I had no idea you felt like that."

"I had you guys on a pedestal." A sky-high one.

"We're human, just like everybody else."

"I see that now." Jenna clutched the phone. Suddenly, she needed an ear. Curt wasn't here, the house was empty and lonely without him and her heart was breaking.

She needed her mom. "Mom, remember I told you about Curt?" she blurted.

"Yes. He's staying at the inn. He's had some problems in his past, right?"

"Right." Jenna took in a trembling breath. "You know that perfection thing I just mentioned?"

"Yes."

"Well, I wanted to emulate you and Dad. I wanted a perfect love. As I told you, Curt has had some problems in his life, and I was letting that keep me from loving him because it all seemed so imperfect." She felt a sob welling up. "Today, he told me he loves me, and I couldn't say it back."

"Oh, wow. It seems a lot's happened since we last spoke." Her mother was silent for a long moment. "Do you love him?"

Jenna swallowed. "Maybe," Jenna said.

"Well, if so, you have to tell him."

"I'm scared to do that," Jenna replied, worrying at a hangnail on her thumb. "Especially after I rejected him today." She sucked in a trembling breath. "What if he can't forgive me?"

"Honey, if he loves you, he'll forgive you."

"I wish I could be sure." Jenna rose and headed for the stairway.

"Nothing in love is for sure."

Jenna started up the stairs. "I know, it's just that after Garrett, I'm so afraid to take a risk."

"Garrett was an unfaithful idiot. I never liked him." Mom sniffed. "Is this man you've met like that?"

"Definitely not," Jenna replied softly yet firmly.

"Curt's the most wonderful, kind and generous man I've ever met."

"Then you have to tell him how you feel."

She reached the top of the stairs. The open door to Curt's room was just a few feet away. "He'll be gone soon, Mom. He told me that he's moving out." Now tears streamed down her cheeks. She swiped at them and eyed the door to his room. "I'm afraid I've ruined it all."

"I guess you have an important decision to make."

"Yes, I do." Probably the most important decision of her life.

"I know you'll do the right thing, honey."

"I hope so."

"Call me and let me know what you decide."

"I will."

"Bye. And, Jenna?"

"Yes?" Jenna whispered.

"I love you."

Jenna smiled shakily. "I love you, too."

The line clicked and went dead. Jenna turned the phone off and stood there in the hall, the ache in her heart remaining, despite her mom's words.

Uncertainty twisted around inside of her until she felt as if her guts were tied in knots.

Curt's open door beckoned, but she couldn't face one more empty room, especially his. So she walked by, staunchly ignoring his space. Instead, she went to her room and started prepping for bed. Though she was pretty sure she wouldn't be sleeping much tonight.

As she washed her face, something occurred to her. Hadn't Jesus's death on the cross freed us from the past? How could she do any less? How could she let Curt go?

All at once, she had to go to his room and face the emptiness waiting there. Maybe that would give her some clarity. She went to the hall. Gritting her teeth, she moved forward and stopped in the entryway to his room. He'd left the bedside light on, and it cast the whole room in a warm, golden glow.

She looked around from the doorway. On the bed lay a duffel bag with clothes folded neatly beside it, as if he'd been packing. Getting ready to leave this place. And her.

He wasn't wasting any time.

Her eyes burned.

Dragging her gaze away from the bed, she noted that his guitar case lay open on the floor next to the flowered easy chair in the corner.

Drawn forward, she went in and moved across the braided rug, sure she could smell his scent hanging in the air. On shaky legs she sat in the chair, wondering if he'd sat here and played the guitar. That thought had her looking down at the guitar in the case by her feet.

She drew her eyebrows together. A piece of folded notepaper sat on the guitar, and as she looked closer, she saw that it had her name written across the front in Curt's neat handwriting.

Breathless, she leaned down, picked up the note and unfolded it with trembling hands. It read:

Jenna—
I'm leaving my guitar for Sam since I know he loves it so much. Please tell him that I will still give him lessons, even though I won't be living here anymore. I was let down a lot as a kid, and I don't want to do that to him, so he can count on me. I promise.
Thank you for everything.
Curt

A tear dropped on the note, leaving a blurred spot where it fell. Jenna pressed a hand to her mouth and let out a little sob, sagging back in the chair.

Oh, my. What a thoughtful, wonderful gesture Curt had made. He was concerned about Sam. Worried about a little boy.

Curt was a truly amazing man.

A man made up of a complicated past, yes. But

also a man transformed in the present by said past, a sum of many things, everything that had happened to him over the years. His traumatic childhood. His wild youth. His misguided years in L.A. His brush with death. His rocky relationship with his father. All of those things had made him the caring, faithful man he was today. The man who was so concerned about a seven-year-old boy's happiness.

The man she loved.

She gave a quick intake of breath.

Yes, yes, yes. She loved Curt. She saw that clearly now. Her fear of heartbreak had held her back, shackled her, kept her from launching herself into his arms earlier today and squealing with delight and telling him she loved him between kisses.

But the fear was gone, chased away by love, by forgiveness.

Forgiveness. She looked up and folded her hands in front of herself. *God, please forgive how judgmental I've been. Curt is a good man, and his past doesn't matter at all. Amen.*

She shot to her feet and the note fluttered to the ground. She had to tell Curt she loved him, right now, before he went one more minute thinking she didn't adore every single thing about him.

But…where was he?

She had no idea. But she'd find him and hope it wasn't too late.

The bottle of Jenna's pain medication sat on the kitchen counter, taunting Curt like a heckler in a crowd.

He looked at the ceiling. His shiner ached and his heart was wounded from Jenna's rejection earlier today.

Lots of stuff hurt. So much so he'd gone to the beach after work and sat there on the sand, alone, wondering if he'd ever be able to return to this house when he knew Jenna didn't want him.

But the stiff Washington Coast breeze and the start of a cold drizzle had finally convinced him he had to go back, if only for the sake of his frozen hands and feet.

But what about his broken heart?

So here he was. Back at the inn. The house was quiet and dark; Jenna had obviously already turned in.

Funny. He'd been hoping in some crazy part of his heart that she'd wait up for him. What a fool he was.

Jenna didn't love him.

His gaze was drawn back to the meds. He could take a pill and forget about his aches and pains for just a little bit.

But the fact remained, no matter what kind of

heroics he'd carried out last night, Jenna couldn't accept his past. He'd done some bad things. She deserved a better man.

His heart throbbed in time with his head, over and over.

He reached out and picked the bottle up. Just one would probably work. Just one and all of his pain would go away.

But…at what price? His self-respect and the hard-won respect of others. His new lease on life, the life he'd dreamed of. Everything he'd worked so hard for since the overdose. Could he really risk all of that for the temporary nothingness the pill would provide?

He called to God from the depths of his soul. *Lord, please help me to resist this temptation, to do the right thing, make the right choice.*

No. He couldn't throw away everything he'd worked for. He'd come so far. He'd be a fool to risk all of that. An absolute idiot. He couldn't go back down the road of his old life.

He wanted a new life. Even if it was a life without the woman he loved. He'd find a way to deal. He was strong enough to do that now. With God on his side, guarding him, guiding him, Curt could do anything.

Just as he started placing the bottle back on the counter, a sound behind him made him turn, the bottle still clutched in his hand.

Jenna stood there in the kitchen doorway. She wore a pair of flannel pants and a green hooded sweatshirt emblazoned with the word *OREGON* in big yellow letters on the front. Her hair was loose around her shoulders.

How could a woman look so perfect?

Her gaze zeroed in on his hand. Eyes widening, she asked, "What are you doing?" Her voice was quiet, but her words packed a punch.

He clenched his jaw. He'd tell her the truth. Honesty would see him through. If not, well, then, she wasn't the woman he thought she was. "My face hurts, so I thought of taking one of these," he said, holding up the bottle. He didn't mention the pain in his heart; that kind of move would be unfair, and that stuff mattered to him now. Especially with Jenna.

She shoved her hands into her sweatshirt pockets, her posture rigid. "But…you didn't." A statement, not a question.

Hope raised its head. "No, I didn't." Man, it felt good to be able to say that.

Her shoulders visibly relaxed. "Why not?"

He set the bottle on the counter. "Because for the first time since I took those pills the night of my overdose, I was smart enough to know it would be a bad idea." He rubbed his eyes. "And because I have too much to live for. God gave me strength to do the right thing."

She moved into the kitchen, her face somber. "You've come a long way."

"Yes, I have." He'd run a marathon, actually. The finish line was close. But he'd be finishing alone.

"You're strong now, and you did the right thing," she said, gathering her hair in one hand. "I'm proud of you."

Her praise made his chest warm. "Your opinion means a lot to me." The world, actually. But he'd keep that to himself, even though he wanted to take her in his arms and tell her he adored her and never wanted to let her go. But that would never happen. She'd made her choice. And it wasn't him.

He noted the shadows beneath her eyes. "Are you okay?"

"Yes, I am now." She paused. "I read your note to Sam."

"Oh, yeah. I wrote it earlier when I was home. Giving Sam my guitar just felt like the right thing to do."

She came closer. The muted kitchen light set her face in shadows, but her eyes were bright, shining with determination. "I have something I need to tell you."

He felt more bad news coming. Maybe about the contents of the letter? "I hope you won't mind me coming here once in a while to give Sam his lessons." He thought about that. "Actually, maybe his mom would let me come to their—"

Jenna reached up and put a finger on his lips. "Shh. Let me talk."

Her touch burned him to his soul. He stilled and remained silent, save for the heavy beat of his heart. "O-okay."

In a quiet voice, she said, "Everyone in my family has a perfect love."

He started to reply.

"Please, Curt, I'd like to finish before you say anything," she said. "It's important."

He pressed his lips tight.

"And I wanted that, too, that perfect love that would last a lifetime."

"But?"

"Well, first, I talked to my mom tonight and discovered that my parents' relationship isn't *actually* picture-perfect."

Concern jabbed at him. "Is everything okay with them?"

"They're having some problems, but they'll work them out. Talking to my mom made me realize that no love is perfect because no person is faultless."

He nodded, barely breathing.

She sucked in a large breath and let it out shakily, closing her eyes for a second. When she opened them, she looked directly at him. "So I wanted the perfect love, and imagine my surprise when I found something better."

Dread pulsed through him, hot and heavy. "You met someone else." Had to be. He wasn't better than her perfect love. Some other lucky guy was.

He clenched his hands at his sides.

She put her hand on his arm. "I can't blame you for saying that because I've been a fool. A complete fool."

He just looked at her, unblinking, unable to speak. But he felt her touch clear to the soles of his feet.

"Luckily for me, I got a clue today when I read that letter. It was the single most profound thing I've ever read."

"Why is that?" he asked in a strangled voice.

Moving still closer, she touched his jaw. "Because it made me realize that I love you, Curt Graham."

His jaw fell into her grasp.

She kept going, both of her hands moving to cradle his cheeks. "I love how concerned you are about Sam, and how you want him to have your guitar, and that you care about not letting him down. And that you risked so much to save us from Sam's father. I love how you've found God and the depth of your faith."

Warmth flooded Curt's chest. "You...love me?"

"Desperately," she whispered, caressing his

face. "You're my perfect man in every way, and I was so hung up on what I thought I wanted that I couldn't see it."

Elated, he put his arms around her and pulled her into his arms. The fresh lemony smell of her hair wrapped around him like a familiar embrace. He held her tight, speechless with joy.

"And then, this morning when you came home, I was downright terrified to risk my heart because of how I'd trusted Garrett, thought he was a good man who would never hurt me, and I'd been so wrong." She lifted her face to Curt's ear. "But I'm not scared anymore. You've proven that you are a strong, honest man with a loving heart, endless faith and a strength of will built upon your trials and tribulations, earned through your past. I want you in my life, forever."

He turned his head and caught her sweet lips with his. He reveled in being lost in the love he felt for her, only her.

Finally he pulled away slightly, just enough to speak. "I want so much to be the man you deserve."

"You are." She smiled, soft and tender. "You're the most wonderful man I've ever known."

His heart swelled. "Hearing you say that makes me feel complete, like I finally have everything I've ever wanted."

"That goes both ways," she replied, tugging him down for another kiss.

With a grin he returned her kiss, pulling her closer. Elation exploded in him, healing his wounds as surely as if God had touched him and declared him whole. Happy. Content.

Loved.

God's handiwork left him humbled.

Thank You, Lord, for a love to last a lifetime. And for always believing I deserved it, even when I didn't believe in myself.

* * * * *

Dear Reader,

I am so glad you joined me for the fifth book set in Moonlight Cove! This series has become very near and dear to my heart, and I love sharing stories about the lives, struggles and faith journeys of the people of Moonlight Cove. Sometimes I wish I lived there, and I hope you do, too.

The idea for Curt had been percolating in my mind since I wrote about his brother Seth in book one. At that time, a hero with a past addiction was just a whisper of an idea, brought about when I read about how many people injure themselves, take pain medications prescribed to them and end up becoming addicted.

I thought featuring a person who struggles with this issue would present a meaty character. Curt had a crisis precipitated by his addiction, and now faces the challenge of not only navigating life post-rehab, but also dealing with the emotional complexity of returning home to face and deal with the disparaging attitudes of others. I wanted to make Curt a character with very real problems who would have to work hard for the things he wanted, most especially love. But I also wanted to create a man who possessed a good heart underneath the veneer formed by his past choices. I wanted him to prove himself to be a man Jenna could love, no matter what had happened in his past, because she eventually sees him as a sum of all of those things in his history, good and bad. He was probably the most difficult character I've ever had to write, but also the most satisfying. I loved giving him his happy ending with Jenna!

Hearing from readers is very fulfilling and it makes all of my work on my books worthwhile. You can contact me at www.lissamanley.com, or at Love Inspired Books.

Many blessings,
Lissa

Questions for Discussion

1. Curt chose to start his new life in Moonlight Cove, and he doubted his chosen path throughout the book. But he kept his goals in mind and continued moving forward. In the end, his choice turned out to be the right one. Discuss a difficult choice that you doubted was the correct one but that turned out to be positive for you overall. How did you cope with your qualms when you weren't sure you'd done the right thing?

2. Jenna wanted an uncomplicated relationship. Was this an unrealistic expectation or was it reasonable, given her past? Why or why not? Discuss if you've had unrealistic expectations in your life, and how that worked out for you.

3. Curt used music as a way to deal with stress, and his singing and guitar playing played a part in drawing him and Jenna together. How has music affected your life? How has it played a pivotal part in a relationship?

4. Jenna and Curt were brought together through shared activities with Sam, and also by the opportunity to reveal their true selves through

their interactions with him. Discuss how a child has bridged a gap between you and someone else. Why do you think people are more likely to open up when a child is involved?

5. At the beginning of the book, Curt hid his addiction from Jenna. Why did he do this? Was it the right decision? Have you ever hidden a part of your past from a loved one? If so, why did you make that decision? Discuss why you do or do not regret your actions.

6. Jenna listened when she heard the ladies at the tea talking about Curt's past. Discuss whether she was wrong to listen in, and why. Was she eavesdropping since she was within earshot and simply stayed put? How else could she have handled this situation? Should she have confronted the women about their gossip? Why or why not?

7. Curt's dad jumped to the conclusion that Curt had stolen the missing pain meds, and accused Curt of the theft in front of others. How could Curt's dad have handled this situation differently? Discuss how you have jumped to an erroneous conclusion in the past and what result

that action ultimately had. Did you regret your hasty judgment? Why or why not?

8. Curt thought that no woman would want him because of his checkered past. Would a past addiction be a deal breaker for you? Why or why not? What are some things in your past that might make someone question a relationship with you? How would you feel if they rejected you because of your past?

9. Curt and his dad had a rocky relationship, yet they managed to reunite in the end when Curt forgave his dad. Would you have done the same thing? Have you ever reconciled with someone who'd wronged you in the past? How did you manage to forgive him or her? Do you regret your decision? Why or why not?

10. Jenna didn't think Curt was the right man for her because of his complicated past. Why did she ultimately change her mind? What precipitated this decision? What did she see in him that prompted her change of heart?

11. Curt was tempted to take some of Jenna's pain medication, yet in the end he realized it was the wrong thing to do. Was this choice credible, given the progress he'd made? Why or

why not? Have you ever come close to making a bad decision? Have you ever stepped back from doing something you knew was probably not the best decision? Discuss.

12. Sam and Curt both had absent parents. Discuss the impact parents have on their kids' lives and how kids turn out as adults. How would your life have turned out if your parents had been different?

13. The scripture in the beginning of the book was Matthew 7:1 and 2—*Judge not that you be judged. For with that judgment you pronounce you will be judged, and the measure you give will be the measure you get.* Discuss what you think this means and how it applies to this story. What application does the scripture have for your life?

LARGER-PRINT BOOKS!

GET 2 FREE
LARGER-PRINT NOVELS
PLUS 2 FREE
MYSTERY GIFTS

Love Inspired

SUSPENSE
RIVETING INSPIRATIONAL ROMANCE

Larger-print novels are now available...

YES! Please send me 2 FREE LARGER-PRINT Love Inspired® Suspense novels and my 2 FREE mystery gifts (gifts are worth about $10). After receiving them, if I don't wish to receive any more books, I can return the shipping statement marked "cancel." If I don't cancel, I will receive 4 brand-new novels every month and be billed just $5.24 per book in the U.S. or $5.74 per book in Canada. That's a savings of at least 23% off the cover price. It's quite a bargain! Shipping and handling is just 50¢ per book in the U.S. and 75¢ per book in Canada.* I understand that accepting the 2 free books and gifts places me under no obligation to buy anything. I can always return a shipment and cancel at any time. Even if I never buy another book, the two free books and gifts are mine to keep forever.

110/310 IDN F5CC

Name _____ (PLEASE PRINT)

Address _____ Apt. #

City _____ State/Prov. _____ Zip/Postal Code

Signature (if under 18, a parent or guardian must sign)

Mail to the Harlequin® Reader Service:
IN U.S.A.: P.O. Box 1867, Buffalo, NY 14240-1867
IN CANADA: P.O. Box 609, Fort Erie, Ontario L2A 5X3

**Are you a current subscriber to Love Inspired Suspense books
and want to receive the larger-print edition?
Call 1-800-873-8635 or visit www.ReaderService.com.**

* Terms and prices subject to change without notice. Prices do not include applicable taxes. Sales tax applicable in N.Y. Canadian residents will be charged applicable taxes. Offer not valid in Quebec. This offer is limited to one order per household. Not valid for current subscribers to Love Inspired Suspense larger-print books. All orders subject to credit approval. Credit or debit balances in a customer's account(s) may be offset by any other outstanding balance owed by or to the customer. Please allow 4 to 6 weeks for delivery. Offer available while quantities last.

Your Privacy—The Harlequin® Reader Service is committed to protecting your privacy. Our Privacy Policy is available online at www.ReaderService.com or upon request from the Harlequin Reader Service.

We make a portion of our mailing list available to reputable third parties that offer products we believe may interest you. If you prefer that we not exchange your name with third parties, or if you wish to clarify or modify your communication preferences, please visit us at www.ReaderService.com/consumerschoice or write to us at Harlequin Reader Service Preference Service, P.O. Box 9062, Buffalo, NY 14269. Include your complete name and address.

LISLPDIR13R